THE HAUNTED B

AND OTHER APPARITIONS

by

Brian Stableford

The Borgo Press
An Imprint of Wildside Press

MMVII

Copyright © 1989, 1997, 2000, 2001, 2002, 2007 by Brian Stableford

All rights reserved.
No part of this book may be reproduced in any form without the expressed written consent of the publisher. Printed in the United States of America.

FIRST EDITION

CONTENTS

About the Author 4
Introduction..5

Seers 7
O Goat-Foot God of Arcady! 20
Chacun sa goule..36
The Haunted Bookshop..41
Beyond Bliss 69
All You Inherit...97
The Will 116
Danny's Inferno 127
Can't Live Without You 134
Community Service..153
Denial 174

ABOUT THE AUTHOR

BRIAN STABLEFORD was born in Yorkshire in 1948. He taught at the University of Reading for several years, but is now a full-time writer. He has written many science fiction and fantasy novels, including: *The Empire of Fear*, *The Werewolves of London*, *Year Zero*, *The Curse of the Coral Bride*, and *The Stones of Camelot*. Collections of his short stories include: *Sexual Chemistry: Sardonic Tales of the Genetic Revolution*, *Designer Genes: Tales of the Biotech Revolution*, and *Sheena and Other Gothic Tales*. He has written numerous nonfiction books, including *Scientific Romance in Britain, 1890-1950*, *Glorious Perversity: The Decline and Fall of Literary Decadence*, and *Science Fact and Science Fiction: An Encyclopedia*. He has contributed hundreds of biographical and critical entries to reference books, including both editions of *The Encyclopedia of Science Fiction* and several editions of the library guide, *Anatomy of Wonder*. He has also translated numerous novels from the French language, including several by the feuilletonist Paul Féval.

The Haunted Bookshop, by Brian Stableford

INTRODUCTION

Ghost stories comprise the most straightforward subgenre of literary accounts of haunting and a considerable category of non-fiction—nowadays mostly in the form of "urban legends". This wide distribution reflects the probable truth of the argument that the idea of the ghost is a highly successful exercise in crude symbolism. What really haunts people, of course, is the past, as preserved in memory, history and myth—or, to be strictly accurate, those aspects of the past that occasion, or ought to occasion, feelings of guilt, shame and remorse.

There is a school of thought which holds that the best accounts of imaginary hauntings are written by people who actually believe in ghosts—or, at least, by people who are capable of pretending such a belief while they are immersed in the process of literary composition. For better or worse, I have never been able to do that; I have insufficient imagination to conjure up any such pretence, even in the altered states of consciousness that are achievable via literary creativity. I must admit to feeling a certain guilt, shame and remorse about this manifest deficiency, and even to being somewhat haunted by it—which is why the title story of the collection features a character who shares my name and existential situation, to the extent of having more fortunate friends. That story and its sequel continued a train of thought set in motion when I was asked to contribute an anecdote to a collection of "true ghost stories" and was forced to improvise something; the anecdote in question, "*Chacun sa goule*", is reproduced here as a preface to "The Haunted Bookshop".

THE HAUNTED BOOKSHOP, BY BRIAN STABLEFORD

The other stories in the collection deal with apparitions of various sorts, five featuring ghosts produced by the troubled consciences of their protagonists and three imagining harassments of a more tangible—and hence more brutal—stripe. One or two of the characters obtain some benefit from the apparitions they experience, reflecting the supposition that it is sometimes good for us to feel guilt, shame and remorse.

Crude Darwinians are compelled to argue that if it were not somehow to the advantage of our genes that we feel guilt, shame and remorse, natural selection would never have provided us with the relevant emotional equipment, but I have never been able to place much credence in or take any comfort from that argument. In most instances, as the vast majority of literary accounts of haunting argue, apparitions do more harm than good, and must therefore be regarded as a heroic mental resistance to the selfish logic of our genes, whose only concern is to urge us to be blindly fruitful and to multiply recklessly. Ghosts do not exist materially, but—perhaps because of their material non-existence rather than in spite of it—they are mostly wiser than that.

"Seers" first appeared in *Gothic Ghosts* (Tor, 1997) edited by Wendy Webb and Charles L. Grant. "O Goat-Foot God of Arcady!" first appeared in *The Silver Web* 15 (2002). "*Chacun sa goule*" first appeared in *Dancing with the Dark* (Gollancz, 1997) edited by Stephen Jones.

"The Haunted Bookshop" first appeared in *Dark Terrors 5* (Gollancz, 2000) edited by Stephen Jones and David Sutton. "Beyond Bliss" appears here for the first time. "All You Inherit" first appeared in *Taps and Sighs* (Subterranean Press, 2000) edited by Peter Crowther. "The Will" first appeared in *Dark Fantasies* (Century 1989) edited by Chris Morgan. "Danny's Inferno" first appeared in *Albedo One* 32 (2007). "Can't Live Without You" first appeared in the December 2001 issue of *Oceans of the Mind*. "Community Service" first appeared in *Terra Incognita* 2 (Spring 1997). "Denial" was supposed to appear in a magazine called *Permutations* whose debut was indefinitely postponed.

The Haunted Bookshop, by Brian Stableford

SEERS

Miss McCann was glad when she saw that the new people in number two had girls. She felt comfortable with girls, but not with boys. She'd been one of three sisters herself, but had never had a brother. In her experience, boys nowadays were rude and worse than rude; Colin from number eleven swore at her constantly, even though he was only ten, and she had a strong suspicion that Terry from number fifteen and his acne-stricken friend Jason from Smallwood Street had been responsible for the break-in she'd suffered last year. In the old days she could have had a quiet word with a young burglar's parents, but these days the parents were as bad as the kids. Terry's Pete and Liz didn't even say hello when they went past, and she'd long since given up saying hello to them. These days, even the people who did return her hellos tended to say it shiftily, as if they'd much rather not.

Mr. and Mrs. Number Two would probably have said hello in their own scrupulous fashion, coming as they now did from the posh side of the street, but they never passed by in a manner that permitted hellos. They were a two-car family—which was only natural, given that number two had recently been converted into a double-garage house—and they never seemed to go anywhere on foot. He had a silver Saab and she had a dark red Citroen. Not that Miss McCann disapproved of that; at least they were sensible cars, not showing-off cars like the ones the last-but one Mr. and Mrs. Number Two had had. She hadn't been at all surprised when they got divorced—but you had to feel sorry for the kids, even for the boy.

THE HAUNTED BOOKSHOP, BY BRIAN STABLEFORD

For the first couple of weeks, Mrs. Number Two ferried the girls to school in the Citroen but then she stopped. By that time Mrs. Forde next door, who knew Mrs. Parris the cleaner, had found out that Mr. and Mrs. Number Two were called Mike and Milly Sandall, and that the girls were Natalie and Gwen. He worked for a firm of building contractors whose offices were in Hammersmith, although he spent a lot of time on sites scattered across three counties; she worked in the Halifax—or what had been the Halifax when it was still a proper building society—in Wokingham. The reason Milly had stopped driving the girls to school was that she had to drop them off half an hour early in order to get to work on time and they'd convinced her that it was safer—or nicer, anyway—to walk there in their own good time than to hang about in the playground.

Miss McCann started saying hello to the girls even before they started walking to school, because they'd always walked back, but it wasn't until she started seeing them mornings as well that they relaxed into the routine of it. She could tell that Natalie was only replying because she'd been brought up to be polite to old ladies, but Gwen actually smiled sometimes. It was easy to see that Natalie was the star of the family and that Gwen walked in her shadow. It wasn't because Natalie was older or prettier, simply that she was star material, while Gwen....

From the very beginning, Gwen reminded Miss McCann of herself. Among Miss McCann's sisters, Linda had been the star while Jennie had been the sergeant-major. Miss McCann didn't know quite how to characterize herself. Being a seer didn't count, because that wasn't a family thing at all; it wasn't something which defined her relationship with other people, merely something within herself.

Miss McCann didn't suspect Gwen of being a seer at first—smiling was no clue at all—but after a while, she began to get an indefinable inkling of it. Maybe it was something in the way Gwen looked round when she and Natalie walked past the graveyard in the shadow of St Anne's, or maybe it was something in the way she faded a little when Natalie criticized her in the presence of other school friends while they were walking home, as Natalie sometimes did when she thought Gwen wasn't being bright enough or brave enough in her manner and her conversation. One way and another, though, Miss McCann soon picked up the impression that Gwen was even more like her than she had thought at first. It didn't bring them together in any measurable way, but there were the smiles, and, if ever Miss McCann saw Gwen when Natalie wasn't with her, there were a few brief words of the kind of conversation which was somehow full even when it was empty.

Miss McCann hadn't known that there was anything to see at number two, of course. She'd been in every odd-numbered house on the street at one time or another, but she'd never been in two, four or six. The odd-numbered houses were two-up-two-downs blocked into a single terrace, and the fact that the neighborhood estate agent had started referring to them as "artisans' cottages" whenever one of them went back on to the market didn't fool anybody; the even-numbered houses had been built between the wars, when commuters and dormitory towns had first been invented, to house people of a very different kind. The two sides of the road didn't mix, except for Mrs. Parris the cleaner. Mrs. Parris had never said anything to Mrs. Forde about goings on, but that wasn't surprising; Mrs. Parris couldn't see for looking, even with her bespectacled eyes. If any of the people who'd occupied number two during the last fifty-odd years had ever seen anything, they'd sensibly kept it to themselves.

It would have been sensible of Gwen to do likewise, and sensible of Miss McCann to let her, but that simply wasn't the way things went. It wasn't anybody's fault.

* * * * * * *

It was only natural, of course, that Gwen should bring her questions to Miss McCann. It wasn't just that she said hello to Miss McCann, and smiled; it was the fact that Miss McCann was the oldest inhabitant of the street—the only rock that had resisted the tides of time and fortune since the dismal days when the street had only had one gently-hissing lamp, fuelled by coal gas, and the middle of the road had been perpetually perfumed by horseshit.

Gwen was subtle about it, of course. She was fourteen, after all. Even in Miss McCann's day, girls who hadn't mastered all the arts of misdirection by the time they hit fourteen were entitled to be regarded as freaks of nature. She began by leaning on Miss McCann's gatepost one warm Sunday afternoon, watching her while she watered the begonias in her window-box. She made five dutifully innocuous remarks before casually springing her trap.

"Did anything ever *happen* in our house, a long time ago?" she asked.

Miss McCann put down the watering-can and wiped her hands on her apron. "What sort of thing?" she asked, although she knew perfectly well.

"Anything. Anything unusual, that is. Natalie heard that there might have been a murder, or a suicide...but she might just have been trying to scare me. She does, sometimes."

Miss McCann was sure that Natalie hadn't said anything of the sort, although that the last part was probably true. Jennie and Linda had often tried to scare her, and had often succeeded.

"No," Miss McCann said, positively. "Nobody was ever murdered in that house, and no one ever committed suicide. If they had, I'd have known about it."

"But somebody must have died there."

"Why must they?"

"It stands to reason," was all Gwen could come up with. "It's been there for ages. Not everybody dies in hospital, even now."

Miss McCann knew perfectly well how many people had died in number two, but she also knew perfectly well that it wasn't a relevant issue. Dad had died in her own house, and had spent an intolerably long time doing it, but she'd never caught a glimpse of him since. Dying in a place obviously had nothing to do with it. Nor had being buried—ghosts were occasionally to be seen in St Anne's churchyard, but they weren't the ghosts of the people in the graves. She had no proof, but she was pretty sure that they were visitors. That didn't signify anything either; when she went visiting, she wasn't mourning or "paying her respects". She wasn't sure what she was doing, but it wasn't either of those things.

Later, Miss McCann reflected that it had been a mistake to think about the graveyard, given the way that one thing could lead to another, but at the time she was thinking about Gwen, and about Gwen being a seer, and about the possibility of helping her just a little.

"I've got to go to St Anne's," she said to Gwen, ducking the question about people who had died in number two. "You can walk with me if you want. I'll just get my coat."

"It's not cold," Gwen pointed out. Gwen wasn't wearing a coat. "Anyway, you've missed church." Mike and Milly didn't go to church, unless you believed what Mrs. Forde said about the Safeways on the trading estate being a Temple of Mammon. They probably went there on Sundays because it was so crowded on Saturdays. Most once-a-week car-shoppers had stuck to their old habits in spite of the relaxation of the Sunday trading laws.

Miss McCann didn't go to church either; it had seemed such a precious freedom to be able to stop, once Dad was gone. That, at least, was one thing Mum had never cared about.

"I'll get my coat anyway," Miss McCann said. "It's just habit. When you get to my age, habits set in. You don't have to come with me if you don't want to."

"I want to," Gwen said. "I want you to tell me about the house—about people who lived in it, a long time ago."

Miss McCann took her coat from the peg. Later, she was to wonder whether she'd hung up her common sense in its place, but at the time she thought she was building herself up to be kind.

* * * * * * *

Miss McCann was careful while they walked along the avenue, and while they walked through the churchyard. Gwen asked a few more leading questions, but she evaded them easily enough. When they got to the graves, though, she immediately took a different tack.

THE HAUNTED BOOKSHOP, BY BRIAN STABLEFORD

"That's my mother and father," she said, pointing out the twin headstones. "That's my Aunt Bet, and over there by the tree's my grandfather Bill Weatherly. There's three more Weatherlys over there, including Bill's brother Fred and his wife, and there's supposed to be a dozen more further over, only the stones have gone. Even gravestones don't last, you know. Everything fades away, given time."

"Why aren't there any more McCanns?" Gwen wanted to know.

"Dad came from Ayrshire, settled here for the work. He was on the canal, then on the railway. Always in transport, he used to say, and never made but one journey in his life. Not true—he was in the war, went to France, was wounded at some place called Chemin-des-Dames.... Primrose Path he always used to call it, the way others used to say Wipers and Passion-dale. He was spotting for the guns, caught a stray shell from behind. Always said he still had shrapnel in his shoulder, but it was just his imagination, and lingering pain that came out in the rain like rheumatism. I never knew what to call it until that war in the Middle East a few years ago. Friendly fire, that's what got him. Didn't stop him outliving mum by twenty years, though—look there, see: died August 4th, 1969. Would have been eighty if he'd hung on till October. Mum was fifty-six. High blood-pressure. Worry, she said. That's got a different name nowadays, too. Stress, they call it. *Dis*tress, I call it. She was a holy terror, was Mum. There's no more room there now, of course. Time was Dad wanted to keep the plot next along, but Jennie wouldn't have it. Jennie was my elder sister—she had three of her own, but they're all grown up. Lives in St Albans. Linda went to Australia, back when it was fashionable. Sends Christmas cards. Linda was the middle one, the pretty one. Probably still is. I bet she dyes her hair."

Gwen endured this long speech with the infinite patience of one well-used to deferring to adults desirous of making long speeches, but she was quick enough to return to her own agenda. "Is there anybody here from my house?" she demanded.

"Not one," Miss McCann was able to tell her, truthfully. "All those Weatherlys were people who stayed put, but there aren't any people who stay put any more. They move on, and on. Everybody in the street bought their houses but me. I'm the only inheritor. Nobody ever lived in my house except my family." She hesitated, but only briefly, before saying: "Sometimes, I think they're still there. Sometimes, I see Mum out of the corner of my eye. Not Dad—but he was a McCann. It's really a Weatherly house, see—around here is the place of the Weatherly dead."

While Miss McCann was driveling on she was looking into Gwen's eyes in search of some sign that she'd touched a chord. What she saw was that she'd been rumbled. Somehow, Gwen knew that she knew. It wasn't as simple as one seer recognizing another, nor as consoling; it was altogether more anxious than that.

"I got Natalie to swap bedrooms," Gwen said, unhappily. "Let *her* see it, I thought. Serve her right. But she never did, and I still did, even though she couldn't possibly have died in *both* rooms. She's following me, and it's not fair. I can't tell Natalie, because she'd laugh, and I can't tell Mum and Dad because they'd make a fuss of *understanding* and send me to the school counselor. I thought at least you might know who she was."

Miss McCann noted that Gwen didn't seem particularly surprised that her elderly neighbor was the kind of person who saw ghosts. She was evidently certain that her parents were the kind of people who didn't, couldn't and wouldn't see ghosts—nor even entertain the possibility of their being seen, in any real sense—but she obviously took it for granted that Miss McCann was cut from commoner, more superstitious clay.

"How old is she?" Miss McCann asked. "Have you noticed what she's wearing?"

"About your age," Gwen told her. "Mostly, she wears dark green. Something heavy, but not thick like velvet. I don't see all of her, but she's not *transparent*, like some people say ghosts are. Not solid, but...well, as if she were *flat*. And there's something weird...you know people say about paintings that their eyes can *follow you round the room*...."

"That would probably be Mrs. Trevithick," Miss McCann interrupted her. "Lived in number two way back, during the second war. Son in the navy, daughter a land girl over Twyford way. Both lived through it, married—daughter right there in that old monstrosity. Nice woman, but always a bit feeble. Thirty years earlier she could have been a full-time invalid, but that wasn't respectable any longer. Nerves was what they called it then. Hadn't invented hypochondria—or if they had, they hadn't told old Dr. Ross."

"Old" Doctor Ross, she remembered with a pang, had been ten years younger than she was now when he had his heart attack. An ugly man, but not as ugly as the "old monstrosity" of a church. She'd never been able to understand why they built it like that when St Luke's over the river had been built ten years earlier and looked much smarter. It hadn't had anything to do with money—something called the Gothic revival. She sometimes heard strangers cooing over it: church-spotters, she always called them, by analogy with the young lads who used to hang over the railway-bridge agitating over engine numbers in the days when the trains ran on steam.

"Did Mrs. Trevithick die in the house?" Gwen asked, still relentlessly barking up the wrong tree.

Miss McCann stared down at her mother's grassy grave. She couldn't remember the time when it had been freshly dug, nor ever having seen flowers on it.

"I've known a lot of people said they'd seen ghosts, Gwen," Miss McCann told her, speaking as softly as she could. "Most of them were fools or liars, but not all. There's others like you and me. Some of them think it's a gift and call it *second sight*, one or two think it's a curse—but they're all just fools, feeding on their own pride or their own fear. The only thing I ever learned from listening to them—the only thing there was to be learned, unless I'm the fool—is that each and every one of them borrowed the stories and the explanations that suited them best, to make sense of what they saw. I can't say whether I'm much different. I like to think that I am, but I dare say the others thought the same. What I can say, though, for sure, is that haunts have nothing to do with murders or suicides, or even deaths in the house. That's all story-telling and dressing up, to make things seem more interesting. It's like fishermen talking about the ones that got away—everything has to be *more so*, or it doesn't seem worth talking about. Everyone who sees ghosts wants to make them more than they are, but if you'll trust the word of an old woman you can take it from me that they're just echoes."

"Echoes?" said Gwen, sounding like an echo herself. She was facing the east wall of the church, and the word bounced back off it, almost as if the old monstrosity had a sense of humor.

"They don't do anything and they don't mean anything," Miss McCann went on. "They're just things left over, which some people can see and others can't, but which don't mean a thing. Understand what I'm saying, Gwen? They can't do you any harm. Flat is what they are, all right: flat like shadows, like rainbows, like the colored sheen on oily rainwater running in the gutter. A trick of the light. There's no need at all to be frightened, and no need at all to tell anyone else what you see, if you don't want to or if you think they won't take it right. It doesn't *mean* anything. It's just echoes."

On the whole, Miss McCann was pleased with the speech. It was the best she could do, and she didn't think anyone cleverer could have done much better. In 1955 or 1935 it might even have worked a treat, but Gwen was a child of a new generation and she probably did Shakespeare at school. Miss McCann looked into the girl's contemplative eyes, and she could see the judgment contained there.

The lady doth protest too much, methinks.

Whenever she hard that line quoted in a TV show, always as a joke, it sent a peculiar shiver down Miss McCann's spine.

"What happened to Mrs. Trevithick?" Gwen asked, still searching for something that would make sense *for her*.

"She and her husband bought a bungalow in Bournemouth," Miss McCann told her. "A retirement home, they call it these days. I never heard any more of them after that. Died long ago, I should think, but not here. Nowhere near here."

"So why is she haunting me?"

Not "haunting the house", Miss McCann observed, but "haunting *me*".

THE HAUNTED BOOKSHOP, BY BRIAN STABLEFORD

"She isn't," Miss McCann told her, trying her damnedest not to protest too much. "She's just an echo. She's not even a *she*, not really. It's an image, not a person. It can't see you, you know. You must believe that. Even if the eyes do seem to follow you around the room, they can't see you. There's no intelligence there, no mind at all. Please believe me, Gwen—I know there are some people who say different, who believe different, but *I know*. It's just something left over from the past, like a piece of old newspaper or a thread of old cotton. You can see her, but she can't see you, any more than she could if she were a photograph you kept on the bedside table."

Trying her damnedest hadn't worked. Perhaps the great looming mass of St Anne's was defeating her dogged attempt to achieve matter-of-factness. She could see Gwen's staring eyes reading between the lines.

Or could she?

After a long pause, Gwen said: "Will I see ghosts wherever I go, from now on?"

"Perhaps," Miss McCann told her, reluctantly. "I don't know. It's said that some people lose the gift, but I don't know."

"A puberty thing, you mean," Gwen muttered. Milly must have talked to her about *puberty things*, as carefully as she could, but Gwen still spoke the words in a shamefaced whisper. She couldn't help it.

"Maybe."

"Are you a miss because you never got married, Miss McCann?" Gwen asked. She blushed as she said it because she knew it might be a direly undiplomatic thing to say, in the circumstances—but she wanted to know, so she blurted it out anyway.

"I've heard it said that some girls lose the gift when they marry," Miss McCann admitted, treading on eggshells. "I think it happens, sometimes. I certainly didn't stay single because I wanted to keep it. I had to look after Dad when Mum became ill, you see. It was expected. Spinsters and maiden aunts were two a penny in those days—it wasn't such an unusual thing to be. Someone had to look after Dad, and I was the one. Jennie was always going to leave home as soon as she could, and Linda...well, she was the pretty one. I was always bottom of the heap, you see: the extra one, the one that turned two's company into three's crowd. My house is only a two-up-two-down you see. We didn't have separate bedrooms like you and Natalie. We were always in one another's pockets, always about one another's business, always running poor Mum ragged and being shouted at, always crammed in like wriggling sardines, always...well, let's just say that you and Natalie have *space*, in a way we never had. You're *separate*, in a way we never were. It's difficult to explain, but it was always going to be the way it was. Someone had to look after Mum and Dad when Mum got ill, and then look after Dad, the way Mum would have if the worry hadn't killed her, and go from spinster to maiden aunt to old maid. Nobody decided—it all just was. It doesn't have anything to do with my being a seer." *Not in the way you mean, anyway*, she refrained from adding.

Gwen digested as much of that as she could, and seemed to have taken some consolation from it. At any rate, she didn't want to dwell on *puberty things* any longer than she had to. She'd grabbed what reassurance she could on that score.

"Are there ghosts in there?" Gwen asked, pointing at the gloomy facade of St Anne's.

"Sometimes I see them out here," Miss McCann said, "but they're nothing to be afraid of. All you have to do is look away. All you'll ever have to do is look away. You don't have to let it make any difference to your life."

Gwen looked up at her, weighing the words; she nearly said something else, but she thought better of it. Perhaps she thought she'd given away far too much already. Miss McCann wondered if she'd still smile next time she said hello.

"Let's go back now," Miss McCann said. "Your parents might be wondering where you've got to." She no longer thought that bringing the girl to the graveyard had been a good idea, but what alternative had she had? Where else could they have gone to talk between themselves, except indoors?

THE HAUNTED BOOKSHOP, BY BRIAN STABLEFORD

* * * * * * *

Later, Miss McCann wondered whether it might have been better to say nothing at all, to have stood her ground in the narrow space between the gate and the door, answering the girl's questions in such a bland way that Gwen would never have guessed. But how could it be better, in the long run, for a girl like that to go on thinking that she was all alone, that she might be mad, or that the ghosts might indeed be haunting *her*? Wasn't it better to offer what reassurances she could? Wasn't it better to try to help her understand?

Such doubts took a little of the taste away from her evening meal, and made it difficult to concentrate on the TV—not that that mattered, given that most TV shows were designed for people who weren't concentrating, especially the ones she habitually watched. It wasn't until she got into her nightdress, though, and took herself off to bed that she really began to worry.

She'll be all right, she told herself. *She's a bright girl, from a sensible family. Things aren't the way they used to be in the old days. She probably has boyfriends already. She certainly has her own space, her privacy. Anyway, kids these days take things in their stride. Drugs at the school gate, computers, holidays in Florida, school counselors, GCSEs. How can a few leftover images, glimpsed from the corner of an eye, get in the way of all that? She can cope. I'll be here to talk whenever she wants to. She'll trust me. In the end, she'll see that what I tell her is the truth, the whole truth, and nothing but the truth. She's bright enough. She'll be all right.*

All the while, Mum was hovering just out of sight, just beyond the scope of the corner of her eye. Miss McCann couldn't see her at all tonight, and she knew perfectly well that what she'd have seen, if she'd seen anything at all, would be just a stray image dislodged in time, just a meaningless trick of the light, whose inescapable gaze was utterly blind, utterly devoid of sense or censure.

Even so, she couldn't help but mutter, as she turned over to face the wall and huddled within her blankets: "It's all right, Mum, I'm not doing anything. I'm not doing anything at all."

The Haunted Bookshop, by Brian Stableford

And even though the house was empty, with nothing left inside it but space, and even though the words were true, and had been for as long as she could remember, she couldn't raise her voice above a whisper.

Even in the soundless privacy of her imagination, she couldn't raise her voice above a whisper.

The Haunted Bookshop, by Brian Stableford

O GOAT-FOOT GOD OF ARCADY!

Laura Crown first caught sight of the face of the Great God Pan in the crowd that had gathered to watch the total eclipse from a hill above Falmouth. The God was staring at her lewdly, his eyes so captivating that once their gazes had locked there was no possible escape.

Laura was astonished, not so much by the fact that the horned and bearded visage should have passed unnoticed by anyone else as by the fact that it had not waited for the moment of darkness to emerge. Had it been born of the passing of the lunar shadow she might have dismissed it as a mere trick of atavistic superstition, but it emerged into the cloud-veiled full sun no more than a minute after the eleventh hour, before she had even raised her dark-lensed glasses to protect her eyes.

The dark lenses did not serve to extinguish the face of the God any more than the light cloud cover hid the fact of the eclipse. Laura tried to look up, as everyone else was doing—and perhaps she succeeded, for she found that she could see the hazy disc of the sun well enough—but she could not avoid the image of the ancient God's insistent eyes. She alone, of all the crowd, was privileged to see a double eclipse, in which the sun's modest light and the moon's shadow were both filtered, with equal efficacy, by the hypnotic eyes of the Arcadian deity.

Pan continued to stare at Laura with avid and uncompromising lust as the black arc cut into the sun's just-visible face at an unexpected angle. Without really thinking about it, Laura had assumed that the eclipse would move horizontally across the face of the sun but that wasn't quite the way it happened. The shadow descended at a subtle angle, which somehow contrived to imply that the whole universe was tilted and that all received ideas might be soon toppled, sent sliding to destruction in a crazy avalanche.

The moment of totality could not banish the unnatural glow of the God's eyes. When the first glimmer of the sun's returning light produced a glimpse of the extravagantly-heralded diamond-ring effect in spite of the thickening cloud, Laura felt that she was indeed betrothed. Having been so long uncommitted to anything other than herself, she now had the Great God Pan's lascivious attention in which to bathe as well as Barnaby's humdrum affections. The slight diminution of temperature that attended the interruption of the sun's light might have seemed like a chill of doubt, as was only to be expected in a woman not far short of forty who had finally decided to tie the knot, but Pan's unexpected presence changed its quality considerably. She was anxious, of course, about entering into a contract with so many unknown and unforeseeable clauses, but if the Great God Pan was prepared to get involved it obviously wasn't any common-or-garden folly.

When the moon had passed on its way and the sun's whole disc was restored the white clouds closed in again, but the face of Pan was still there, etched into the white vapor as if the God had ascended from the crowd on the hill into his Olympian heritage. It was a long time since Laura had studied classics at university, and she was glad to find that sixteen years in the advertising business hadn't entirely cut her off from its imaginative heritage.

"Wasn't it awesome?" Barnaby said to her, re-emitting the sentiment that had been drilled into his scientifically-tempered but nevertheless malleable soul by media hype. "Wasn't it lucky that the cloud parted, just in time? Aren't you glad we came?" Somehow, that kind of forced enthusiasm didn't seem entirely becoming in a medical man—even one who had sold out to big business in order to fund his biotechnological researches and provide him with the means to marry in some sort of style.

Laura thought about the interminable drive from London and the even-more-interminable drive back that still lay ahead of them. Although it was their first holiday together since the engagement they had agreed that the whole enterprise would have to be packed into three days, in order that they could both be back at work on Thursday.

"We'd have got a better view watching TV," she said. "Or in Roumania."

"The trouble with you hard-bitten career women," Barnaby told her, "is that you've squeezed all the romance out of your souls. Just because you've turned a deaf ear to the ticking of the proverbial biological clock, it doesn't mean you have to be oblivious to all the wonders of nature."

Laura wasn't sure that she had turned a deaf ear to the proverbial clock in question, and she certainly wasn't sure that she wanted Barnaby to take it for granted that she had, but the fact that she had accepted his proposal without demanding any preliminary discussion of such issues had wrong-footed her, and she knew that it wouldn't be easy to introduce such matters now without running the risk of upsetting the entire apple-cart.

"I'm not oblivious to the wonders of nature," she assured him, drawing upon her practiced skill in off-the-cuff wordplay, "but eclipses are like sex—no matter how much trouble you go to in order to get the circumstances right, it's always over in a matter of minutes."

* * * * * * *

While they were stuck in a tailback at Okehampton Laura asked Barnaby whether genetic engineers would ever be able to create chimeras like the satyrs of Greek mythology. He was always glad to have an opportunity to further her education.

"We're already more than half way there," he reported. "Technically, it'll be possible to produce designed chimeras in ten or fifteen years—twenty at the most. We won't be crossing humans with other species, of course. There's no demand to take us through the ethical barriers. Entirely human chimeras are a different matter."

Laura didn't understand, at first, why the notion of an "entirely human chimera" wasn't a contradiction in terms.

THE HAUNTED BOOKSHOP, BY BRIAN STABLEFORD

Surely, she argued, an entirely human being couldn't qualify as a chimera at all.

"Not at all," said Barnaby. "It's just an inversion of the twinning process. A Polish embryologist named Kristof Tarkowski reasoned way back in the fifties that if early embryos could split to produce identical twins, there was no reason why cells from two separate embryos couldn't fuse into a single individual, producing a genetic chimera. He did it *in vitro*, using mouse embryos, in 1961—by which time the search for natural human chimeras was under way. Chimerical individuals are usually indistinguishable from others of their kind, although mouse chimeras are recognizable if, for instance, each of the original embryos carries a gene specifying a different fur-color, in which case the resultant patchwork gives the game away. The most obvious naturally-produced chimeras are formed by the fusion of embryos of different sexes, although it's unusual for those to result in live births."

"Did they find any natural human chimeras?" Laura wanted to now. "Were they hermaphrodites?"

"Most hermaphrodites aren't chimeras," Barnaby said, with characteristically dutiful pedantry. "Human intersexes are usually produced by abnormal embryonic development. The hundred or so human chimeras located by genetic analysis during the last forty years have almost all been anatomically normal. There must be hundreds of thousands within the unanalyzed population of Europe and America. There'll soon be more, of course, when demand begins to pick up."

"Why? What demand?"

"The demand from same-sex couples. At present, the children born to lesbian couples by donor insemination are only related to their birth-mothers, but IVF allows for the possibility of fertilizing eggs from both mothers with the donor sperm and then fusing two embryos into a chimera, so that the resultant child is genetically related to both social parents. Two male homosexuals could donate sperm to fertilize eggs of a single donor mother, which can then be fused to create an embryo with two fathers. Although they involve a third genetic parent, chimeras are much easier to produce than two-parent embryos in which a set of chromosomes has had to be transplanted from a sperm into a denucleated egg, or from an egg into a denucleated sperm, so they'll probably be the preferred option in the short term. In the longer term, of course—when longevity technology requires severe population control and large groups of adults will have to form collective households for the purpose of child-rearing—it should be possible to produce chimerical children with at least eight parents, always providing that careful selection can screen out potential incompatibilities. That shouldn't be terribly difficult, given that interspecific chimeras have already been produced. Families of cells that share the same womb and respond to the same developmental signals tend to get along far better in adult life than the cells of transplanted organs and those of a host body."

"Have interspecific chimeras been produced already?" Laura asked. It was news to her, although she had taken care in the early days of their relationship to scan through Barnaby's subscription copies of *New Scientist*. It had seemed important then to obtain the brownie points available for taking an interest in his vocation. Perhaps it was even more important now that the ring was on her finger, given that they intended to spend the rest of their lives together.

"The first one created *in vitro* that got a good deal of publicity was the dear old geep," Barnaby told her. "That one was derived by combining the embryos of a goat and a sheep. It was a random patchwork, but it functioned well enough even as a adult and it was reasonably photogenic—much more so than that damn mouse with the human ear on its back. That one probably set the cause back ten years, and it wasn't even a genuine chimera!

"As we learn more about the chemical signals that control the development of the embryo it should become possible to make sure that the cells of one genetic parent respond selectively, thus producing designed chimeras. I doubt that it will ever be practical to produce an individual with the front end of a lion, the midriff of a goat and the hindquarters of a lizard, but satyrs would be a lot easier, if there were any reason to make them. A satire performed by real satyrs would be something to see, but I can't quite see us getting the project past the Ethics Committee."

THE HAUNTED BOOKSHOP, BY BRIAN STABLEFORD

Fortunately, the traffic cleared up before Exeter and the motorway didn't become jammed again until they were approaching Basingstoke. All in all, Barnaby assured her—taking in the cloud-obscured eclipse and the recent formalization of their relationship as well as the driving conditions—it had all gone as well as could be expected. Laura had no real reason to suspect otherwise.

* * * * * * *

Laura had been followed and spied on before, but never with any real application, let alone total obsession. It was as if the difficulty she had always had in shopping for men of what conventional retailing jargon called "merchandisable quality" had cut right across the social spectrum, so that even her stalkers had turned out to be commitment-phobic. Once the Great God Pan got on to her case, though, it was a different matter.

There were no funny phone-calls, but she would catch glimpses of the God's face at all the most expectable moments, on the crowded platform at Baker Street tube-station, among the gawkers who gathered at the road traffic accident at the junction of Marylebone Road and Gloucester Place, and in the ticket-agency queue in Newport Street. Pan was always a pedestrian, never a driver, but that was hardly surprising. Oddly enough, she soon began to catch sight of him in crowd scenes in movies and studio audiences on TV, from which it shouldn't have been possible for him to look out at her and catch her eye—but he was a God, after all. If the Great God Pan couldn't look out of a cinema or a TV screen at someone in the audience, who could?

Pan's appearances were not limited by the hour of day. Laura was just as likely to catch sight of him at nine in the morning as at nine in the evening. They were, however, affected by the quality of the light. His gnarled features were far more likely to appear at the very edge of a building's shadow than they were in deep shadow or full glare. Laura's regular habits and exact timetabling rarely exposed her to the dawn's early light, but she was often abroad in the twilight, which crept towards the margins of the working day as August gave way to September and the end of British Summer Time moved gradually closer. The God was no more likely to appear at or after sunset than at any other time, but whenever he did it was always to take advantage of some whimsical trick of the fading light. Although he was always far too serious to wear a smile, red sky at night always seemed to stain his features with a strange kind of delight.

Laura had never been unduly frightened by the prospect of being stalked or the suspicion that it was actually happening to her. It had always seemed to her to be an inherently unpleasant experience, but not one that warranted extreme anxiety. She had taken lessons in self-defense, and had applied them with ruthless efficiency on several past occasions to drunken lechers and potential bag-snatchers. The first and most important lesson to be learned, her instructor had told her, was not to panic. Her instructor had not, of course, envisaged the possibility that any of his pupils would ever encounter the original author of panic, but Laura found that the advice still held good even where the Great God Pan was concerned. She didn't actually get to *like* being stalked by Pan, but she wasn't terrified by it either.

Presumably, her ability to resist panic had as much to do with Pan's polite reluctance to force it upon her as with her own inner fortitude, but the end result was that she eventually ceased to be alarmed or intimidated by the glimpses of his face that she caught. He didn't seem to pose much of a threat. His features were lewd, to be sure, and his gaze invariably testified to the fullness of his carnal appetite, but Laura didn't feel as if she were in danger of rape or any other violent disaster. Having recognized her admirer—she could not bring herself to think of him as an adversary or an enemy—she quickly became accustomed to his inconstant but unceasing presence.

Laura was required to exercise a certain amount of discretion whenever Pan appeared while she was with Barnaby, but that wasn't unduly difficult. Although Barnaby frequently accused her of being absent-minded, and even of not listening to a word he said, he was the one more prone to be mentally AWOL and self-preoccupied—with far less excuse, given that her professionally-honed conversation was generally wittier and much more interesting than his. Barnaby never noticed when his fiancée's wandering attention was suddenly caught by the sight of the God's voluptuous lips and leering eyes. Never once did he say "What is it?" or "What's the matter?" It made no difference whether they were eating out in Gerrard Street or sprawling on one or other of their leather sofas watching TV. He simply didn't have the motivation to get fully to grips with her experiences and feelings.

Pan made no more discrimination between Barnaby's presence and Barnaby's absence than he did between the hours of daylight and the dead of night, although the moments of his appearance did tend to favor the margins and transitions of the engaged couple's relationship. On the rare occasions when Laura took the trouble to wonder whether Pan's visitations might be hallucinatory she sometimes considered the corollary hypothesis that he might be a symptom of the fact that her relationship with Barnaby was still so full of uncertainties. Sometimes, she wondered whether it might be winding down before they even reached the altar, their eventual separation and divorce taking shape within the as-yet-undelivered embryo of their union. One of the side-effects of her chosen profession, however, was a healthy contempt for pop psychology, so she wasn't tempted to follow such trains of thought too far.

Laura eventually decided that Pan's presence was just a new fact of life, neither to be welcomed nor deplored. Just because he was there, and apparently hell-bent on sticking close to her, there was no more reason to give way to dismay than there was to fall down and worship him. It was 1999, after all, and Gods didn't count for much any more, even if it had turned out that widely-publicized reports of their death had been somewhat exaggerated.

* * * * * * *

"Given that they have to form in the same womb," Laura said to Barnaby, while they were tucking into crispy duck at the Peking Palace, "I suppose natural chimeras have to be all of one species. All the old jokes about crossing kangaroos and sheep to get woolly jumpers are nonsensical."

"Right," said Barnaby. "Mind you, Brimster's work has opened up some intriguing possibilities."

"Who's Brimster?"

"Ralph Brimster, University of Pennsylvania Veterinary School. He pioneered a new method of infertility treatment for men who can't produce spermatids, let alone motile sperm. What you do is to take the most elementary stem cells from the testicles—spermatogonia—and transplant them into the testicles of a pig or a sheep. The host tissues take over the production process, so that the boar or ram produces human sperms along with its own. You can separate them by centrifuge and use the human ones in standard IVF procedures. The applications are limited at present because there are so few patients in the relevant category—but the more fanciful corollaries of the method tend towards the bizarre. In theory, a single host animal could produce sperms from the transplanted spermatogonia of a dozen or a hundred donors, of as many different species. Add in the complementary technology and you have some really wild scenarios."

"What's the complementary technology?" Laura asked, as she was obviously being invited to do.

"Same theory, different sex. Not quite as simple, though. Male animals produce sperms continuously from puberty until death, or at least until their balls weaken. Females are born with their entire stock of oocytes already in place—the cells that survive to the onset of ovulation have already survived considerable attrition, and the spares continue to die while their lucky neighbors are launched at monthly intervals on their journey to the uterus. If you want to transplant stem cells into a female, you have to do it into a fetus. On the other hand, we're already battling the Ethics Committees for the right to strip oocytes out of aborted female fetuses to use as donor eggs in IVF treatments for infertile women—it saves using invasive methods on adult volunteers—so there's a window of opportunity there if we can ever get permission to go through it."

"Let me get this straight," Laura said, as she used her chopsticks to pluck sizzling lamb from the lazy Susan and dump it into her rice-bowl. "In theory, you could engineer a male animal to produce sperms of a dozen different species, which could then be let loose in a Petri dish with a mess of equally-mixed egg-cells produced by an aborted fetus—and some of the resultant embryos could be fused, if some interested genetic engineer cared to do it."

"In theory," Barnaby agreed. "But it's not genetic engineering, in the strict sense. Creating chimeras is actually easier than creating transgenic animals—except for the small matter of controlling the patchwork to produce a particular phenotypic design. That's a hurdle we're not quite ready to jump. Twenty years, maybe—ten if there were a more obvious commercial application than producing new kinds of pets. It's a pity Mother Nature didn't take care of that herself. Maybe there are other worlds where evolution employs chimerization to shuffle the genetic deck as well as sex, but it would probably be limited to invertebrates and egg-layers. Mammalian mothers probably wouldn't be able to stand the strain—or, of course, the uncertainty."

Laura thought about that for a few minutes before saying: "I suppose we're certain that Earth's biosphere never experimented with that kind of thing."

"How could we ever be certain?" Barnaby countered. "Fossils don't leave much for genetic analysis. *Jurassic Park* is pure fantasy, and even if it weren't we'd have no chance of figuring out exactly what made ammonites or trilobites tick. Given that there are so many natural chimeras about, it's possible that they've played some role in natural selection, but the overwhelming likelihood is that it was only within species. Mother Nature could never have mastered the art of transplanting spermatogonia, let alone oocyte-generating stem cells. For that you'd need a God—or a really hot biotechnologist."

He had to stop then in order to concentrate on the serious business of loading his rice-bowl. Considering that he was supposed to be a dab hand with a micropipette, guiding recalcitrant sperms into the nuclei of ova while peering down a microscope, Barnaby was amazingly cack-handed when it came to using chopsticks.

The Haunted Bookshop, by Brian Stableford

* * * * * * *

It was not long before the Great God Pan began to invade her dreams. Laura had always been a good sleeper, always able to forget her dreams as soon as she woke up, so it was possible that Pan had been in them for some time before she became aware of him—perhaps forever—but it wasn't until she was hit by the misfired rocket at the firework party on November 5th that she became fully aware of his presence.

The burns on her arm and neck weren't bad, and she was assured that they'd heal without any conspicuous scarring, but they were naggingly painful and Laura couldn't resist the temptation to give her nightly dose of ibuprofen a helping hand with a couple of stiff vodkas. It wasn't entirely surprising that she slept fitfully, or that her dreams were mildly disturbing.

If it had just been a matter of glimpsing Pan's leering face the way she did when she was awake the dreams wouldn't have qualified, even marginally, as nightmares—but there was more to them than that. In the dreams, Pan often became confused with his more sinister kin: with the Devil, who had borrowed his shaggy legs, horns and cloven feet, and with Shub-Niggurath, the legendary goat with a thousand young. Laura had read a good deal of Lovecraft in her teens, and although she hadn't thought about it for twenty years she now began to recall that the monstrous Great Old Ones had been somewhat given to experiments in miscegenation that had left contemporary mankind with various chimerical stigmata, including the Innsmouth Look. All that was fantasy, of course—the Devil too—but her classical education had taught her that all effective fantasy captured something of the spirit of its time as well as pushing buttons buried deep in the human psyche.

In her dreams, Laura often had to remind herself that the Devil and Shub-Niggurath were "only Pan in disguise", although that didn't seem like such a saving grace when she remembered that Pan had his sinister side too. Oscar Wilde's poem might have implored the return of the "goat-foot god of Arcady" to wonder-starved Victorian England and Aleister Crowley might have tried his utmost to summon the deity to the twentieth century, but such yearnings were textbook examples of the old adage that you should be careful what you wish for in case you get it.

In her dreams, Pan came much closer to Laura than he ever did in the London streets or ever could when he merely peeped out of a TV image. In her dreams she could hear the scrape of his misshapen feet as they scraped on bare floorboards and she could smell the musky odor of his hairy body. Sometimes, she felt the warmth of his heavy breath on the nape and side of her neck, stinging the spot where the rocket had struck her a glancing blow. The implicit eroticism of his presence was always muted, though. Now that she was with Barnaby she had little or no occasion to feel literally frustrated, and the raw discomforts that troubled her sleep were more elementary than that.

By the time November gave way to December and her waking thoughts had to take account of Christmas and the false Millennium Laura's burns had healed and she was sleeping more soundly again, but the legacy of her nocturnal encounters lingered and she couldn't seem to recover the art of forgetting her dreams as soon as she awoke.

She asked Barnaby whether it was possible for a goat to bear a thousand young and he said that although it had never been possible before it was now, because you could strip the oocytes from the aborted fetus of a goat and freeze them in liquid nitrogen, releasing them ten or a hundred at a time to be fertilized *in vitro* before being implanted into the wombs of any number of surrogate nannies. When she asked him in the Tut'n'Shive on Upper Street, in between two stand-up comedians' open mike spots, whether there wasn't something slightly spooky—nightmarish, even—about a goat with a thousand young *which had never been born itself* he told her that of course there wasn't.

"If you were to become pregnant," he said, rather awkwardly—perhaps because he was very conscious of the fact that they had not even discussed the prospect of attempting to have children, before or since he had suggested that they get married—"you'd not only be carrying your daughter within you, but all the oocytes which might one day become your maternal grandchildren. It's amazing, but it's not spooky. It's the way things are, replete with opportunity. Now that we know how the processes of reproduction work, biotechnologists can see a whole spectrum of new opportunities that are already built into the system whether Mother Nature ever bothered to use them or not. We biotechnologists have to seize those opportunities, if we're to make the most of ourselves. We ought to seize them all."

Then he blushed, as if he might have assumed or said too much.

* * * * * * *

By the time he'd sunk his fifth pint and started on his sixth, Barnaby was waxing exceedingly lyrical about the possibility that the evolution of life on Earth must have involved the seizing of any and all opportunities that came along, even if a few of them had been shelved for millions of generations.

"Maybe chimerization hasn't played much of a role in evolution for the last few hundred million years," he conceded, "but if you go way back, there are some obvious contenders. Lichens are chimerical, and it may be that all multicellular organisms arose, in the first instance, by chimerization. The chloroplasts in plant cells and the mitochondria in animal cells must have started out as distinct organisms, and you could make out a case for creatures like the Portuguese man-o'-war being chimerical rather than colonial—but the real clincher, it seems to me, is metamorphosis. What's an insect, after all, but a serial chimera? The genetic blueprint for making a larva must have been separate, once upon a time, from that for making a fly or a beetle. How did they come together to form an organism that could exploit the best features of both designs as the seasons changed? The adaptive radiation of all the major invertebrate groups must have involved chimerization as well as natural selection. If only our ancestral line had preserved the ability long enough, there might have been such things as werewolves."

"But there aren't," Laura pointed out. "No werewolves, no satyrs, no gorgons, no centaurs. There aren't, and presumably never were." She didn't know whether she was teasing or testing. She had sunk enough vodkas on her own account that even the would-be comedian who was just surrendering the mike seemed like a fabulous creature of sorts, having just told three mother-in-law jokes delicately tinted in blue.

"No, there never were," Barnaby agreed, "and maybe never will be—but the human imagination is less foolish than we sometimes think. Give me twenty years and a big enough grant and I could make you a satyr. Give me forty, and an Ethics Committee as blind as justice, and I could make you the grandmother of a satyr whose mother was never born. Give me a goat to help me out, and I could be father to a thousand young."

Laura looked at him long and hard then, and said: "Is that a subtle way of telling me that you're infertile?"

There was no one at the mike telling inept jokes, but the noise of the pub was still slightly hushed. Laura glanced at the empty makeshift stage, as if expecting to see the Great God Pan peering around the velvet curtain, weighing up the audience in advance of pitching into his brand new act.

"Would it matter?" Barnaby asked, gruffly. "Given that there's so much that can done about it nowadays?"

"No," she said, mildly. "It wouldn't matter to me, even if there weren't anything to be done. It's not a major issue. I'm not getting married because I'm desperate to conceive before it's too late. That's never been a factor. Would it matter to you?"

"It used to," he said, faintly. "Not any more. I should have told you, I suppose, but it never came up. Not a major issue, as you said. Even so...."

"It doesn't matter," she told him, flatly. "And if it did...as you say, there are things that can be done about it. Not spooky things. Just opportunities. Is that why you were so interested in Brimster's work?"

"It helped," he admitted.

"So now you've told me," she said, "and nothing's changed."

"No," he admitted. "Nothing's changed. Except that...we think we just grow, Laura, but we don't. We think we just get bigger for a while, then wrinklier, always remaining essentially the same, but we don't. Even those of us who aren't natural chimeras carry the legacy of ancient chimerizations in our genes. It cuts far deeper and last far longer than the ghostly gills our embryos grow and then discard. We're not as pure or as simple as we think we are. We undergo metamorphoses of our own, inwardly as well as outwardly. We can't always tell what we'll want tomorrow, and even though everyone who can do arithmetic knows that the Millennium won't end until next December, the numbers on the big clock will still take a big tumble as 1999 gives way to 2000. Sometimes, things creep up on you when you least expect them."

"Sure they do," she agreed. Alcoholic eloquence had confused him as well as helping him to get it all off his chest, but Laura had no difficulty in grasping the gist of his argument. She was, after all, supposed to be expert in the art of designing and decoding subtexts. "But they're not necessarily nightmarish, even if they're not entirely pleasant. As you said, the human imagination isn't as foolish as some people think."

* * * * * * *

After that, Laura soon began to forget her dreams again. She didn't doubt that she had them, just as everybody did, but they didn't make enough impact on her to turn themselves into memories. It was only in reality that she had to cope with the Great God Pan, and in reality he never threatened to turn into the Devil, or the goat with a thousand young. In reality, he simply maintained his vigil, following her when she went to work and following her when she returned, keeping track of her while she was with Barnaby and keeping track of her when she was alone. She was sure that he was always there, on every street and in every TV show, sometimes letting her catch sight of him and sometimes staying out of view.

When he saw that she had begun to take him for granted Pan became bolder. The distance between them lessened day by day as the new year approached and dawned—attended by only a few of the much-heralded petty disasters—and

Laura knew that it was only a matter of time before they actually touched. She didn't know when, at first, but she thought that she could guess where and how, and with those anticipations in mind she could be patient. She had seen the face of Pan upon the shadowed moon as it eclipsed the sun and she would not be frightened to see it in the shadowed eyes of her husband-to-be, momentarily eclipsing his consciousness. That would neither be the end of the matter, nor a new beginning, but it would be a consummation of sorts.

It was, Laura knew, in the *Metamorphoses* of Ovid that the tale was told of Pan's loving pursuit of the nymph Syrinx, who had been content in the end to be turned into his instrument, becoming the means by which he made his music. As a career woman and a feminist she could not be expected to admire such stupid passivity, but she knew that the sensible solution to that particular dilemma was to become a collaborator in the making of the music, not to refuse to make music at all. Perhaps, she thought, Syrinx really had been a collaborator, or even the true author of the music that Pan played, while Pan had played a greater part in other aspects of their life. He might have been the God, the Creator, but that did not mean that he alone had responsibility for what he made.

In fact, as Laura might and perhaps would have guessed had she not thought it far too hackneyed and twee, it was on the night of their wedding, as their honeymoon in Madeira began, that she finally made sensitive contact with the Great God Pan. She saw his face within the face in which it had always belonged, albeit slightly clouded by a mist of mild intoxication and long-suppressed anxiety. Pan looked at her with a lust that was anything but new, but far from jaded, and although he didn't smile, there was a strange delight in his sunset-lit expression.

"Everything can still be done," said the Great God Pan, as they celebrated together. "There's no necessity, but everything that isn't possible now will be possible soon enough. The old limitations simply don't apply any more."

"I know," she said. "And I'm glad."

THE HAUNTED BOOKSHOP, BY BRIAN STABLEFORD

CHACUN SA GOULE

We are all haunted. The dead are all around us, in substance and in spirit. Every breath we take draws in carbon atoms that were once incorporated into the bodies of other men; with every mouthful of food we engulf the remains of our ancestors. As we devour them they devour us, fueling the slow fire of life—the fire whose ashes are absorbed, in the end, into the earth and her fruits, or lost on the wings of the wind.

Our inescapable fate is to be eaten and breathed in our turn.

Once we are conscious of the everpresence of the dead we can easily feel their nearness. To see them, and to hear their voices, is only a little more difficult—but that is not the essence of being haunted. We are not haunted because we sometimes see invisible ghosts, or hear their inaudible words; we are haunted because, in our imagination, *they see us*. In seeing us, even though their sight is imaginary, they know our inmost thoughts.

We have no secrets from the dead.

Those of us who seek to avoid our ghosts cannot win free of them by mere denial. We may narrow our field of view to brute facts and causal explanations, refusing the commitment of belief to everything save evidence and natural law, but our experience of the world remains stubbornly magical. Fear and desire color everything we see and hear; we cannot observe things as they are without knowing what they might be. Meaning is everywhere in the human world, and meaning is a heritage: the gift of ghosts.

Those of us who hope that we are wise do not try to avoid our ghosts. We try, instead, to choose them: to select

The Haunted Bookshop, by Brian Stableford

from the infinite mazes of shadow those precious shades with which we would like to become more intimately acquainted.

Novelists and historians are no more haunted than anyone else, in the passive sense, but by taking an active part in their own haunting they may make better contact with individual phantoms. The characters that novelists and historians create—and historians do create their characters, albeit in imitation of people who once lived and breathed—are not ghosts themselves but they are very like ghosts in certain significant ways. They are seen too clearly and heard too plainly, but they have the same facility that ghosts have for being there when they are not, for seeing and hearing us without the need of eyes and ears. Most importantly of all, characters are built out of materials borrowed from the world of ghosts.

All fictions are ghouls, fed according to the cannibal habit on the icons of the dead.

I cannot name all the ghosts that I have welcomed across my inner threshold, although I recognize most of them. Nor can I tell you where I met them all—although I am happy to agree with the common opinion that they are most often met by night, in lonely places. I do not frequent graveyards at midnight, but I am sure that if I did I would find ghosts therein, and would feel their nearness much more sharply than I feel it when I am surrounded by the glamour of artificial light and the clamor of the living. I do frequent libraries, at all hours, and that might account for the fact that my most intimate relationships are with the ghosts of writers.

I dare say that H. P. Lovecraft was right when he said that the most fearful and powerful ghosts lurk between the lines of forbidden books, the most ominous of which would be the Book of the Names of the Dead (although I fear that the names in question must have lost at least some of their force in being translated from the Arabic to the Latin). I, like most of us, have had to be content with permitted books, but I have found them to be not without a certain power. I have been fascinated by the shade of Lovecraft, but far more deeply enraptured by the spirit of his friend, Clark Ashton Smith. For wit and world-view there is no ghost more eloquent to me than Oscar Wilde, but for intensity and intrigue I put the highest value on visitations from further afield. The ghosts which haunt me most efficiently and most effusively are French. I have no idea why this is, but an element of the unknown and the unknowable is indispensable to any halfway decent haunting.

I wish that Charles Baudelaire had once appeared in my study—wearing no colors but black, as he did in life—to fix me with his stern and disapproving glare. I wish that in some careless reverie I had once been swept aside in time and space to the rue des Saints-Pères at the turn of the century, there to confront the lupus-scarred face of Rémy de Gourmont. I wish that Anatole France had once dropped a skeletal hand on my shoulder as I negotiated some narrow corridor steeped in Stygian shadow. But if any of these things had ever happened, I would not write about it here. It would be irreverent to turn such an experience into a mere anecdote. I am, however, prepared to offer one absolutely true example of the supernatural at work.

On 4 May 1996 I delivered the last batch of entries that I had done for John Clute's *Encyclopedia of Fantasy*. It included an entry on Maurice Maeterlinck. In the course of writing that entry I had come across a reference to a fantasy play called *Joyzelle* (1903), of which I had never heard, although I thought I knew the author's work tolerably well. On May 17 I was visiting a couple of second-hand bookshops in Bristol when I came across a temporary AA road-sign pointing the way to an Antiquarian Book Fair, of whose staging I had been entirely ignorant. One of the stalls therein had a shelf of books in French, which I naturally examined with care. There I found a copy of *Joyzelle*—which actually should not have been there, because it was the English translation by Alexander Texeira de Mattos (who was, of course, the second husband of Oscar Wilde's brother's widow).

There are people in the world who would flatly refuse to consider this incident supernatural, dismissing it as mere coincidence. Within the calculus of rationality they would doubtless be deemed correct but we writers are experts in the business of coincidence. We know that, in terms of their literary functions, there is no difference at all between the impossible and the unlikely; they are invoked at exactly the same points in a narrative for exactly the same purposes.

When the machine of a plot has stalled and requires kick-starting, we writers use coincidence or the supernatural without conscience or discrimination, and when we need a climax that will excite, inspire and astonish we reach with equal alacrity for the spectacular million-to-one-shot or the flamboyant miracle. Mundane existence is, of course, full to overflowing with mere coincidences, but within the context of a plot no coincidence is *mere*; each and every one of them is significant, meaningful and supernatural. Within the narrative of my life—which I am composing day by day as carefully as I can—there can be no doubt that I have not only met the ghost of Maurice Maeterlinck but have received a little kindly guidance therefrom.

Some readers, I suppose, will regret that my ghostly encounter was not scarier, or (at the very least) funnier. As I have already said, though, haunting is something that goes on all the time; life as we know it would not be possible without it. If meaning is the gift of ghosts—as it is—we ought to hesitate before giving too free a rein to the corrosive ingratitude which insists that all ghosts are horrid. All ghosts are, admittedly, ghoulish—but we are ghoulish ourselves if we are honest enough to see and say it; the carefully-cooked food on which we dine every day is compounded from the remnant atoms of the legions of the dead.

The French historian Jules Michelet, of whom it was said that no other historian ever cared as little for accuracy, was scrupulously correct in his estimation of himself. "I have drunk too deep," he wrote—sadly, one presumes—"of the black blood of the dead."

I have drunk of that black blood too, and so have you—but I wonder if either of us has truly *tasted* it, savoring its implications to the full. Perhaps we should both try harder.

You will not choose the same ghosts as I from the multitude which passes you by; you will doubtless claim your own, for your own reasons. It is not for me to ask who they are, or where you meet them, or what appearances they offer to you. Such things are private, and perhaps best kept so. But if I may presume to offer you a little advice, I beg you to let your chosen ghosts take their proper roles within the narratives of your lives. Neither deny nor diminish them; do not say that they do not exist, and do not dismiss their manifestations as mere hallucinations and coincidences. They are precious, both as levers to move the plot of your existence whenever it is stalled, and as aspects of the climax that your life will inevitably require.

Listen to your ghosts; learn from your ghosts; devour your ghosts as they devour you, with unashamed ghoulishness.

Every time I dream about Charles Baudelaire or Oscar Wilde, I awake hopeful that I might find beside my pillow a tear-stained copy of *Les Fleurs du mal* or a fresh green carnation. Were any such thing to happen I would never tell a soul; too many stories have already ended that way and we should all do our level best to transcend the limits of cliché—but if it were to happen, I would be grateful.

I feel that I have not yet drunk deep enough of the black blood of the dead, nor tasted every flavor it has to offer.

THE HAUNTED BOOKSHOP, BY BRIAN STABLEFORD

THE HAUNTED BOOKSHOP

I was putting the final touches to the introduction to a new edition of C. D. Pamely's *Tales of Mystery and Terror* when the phone rang. I picked it up with my left hand while my right forefinger finished pecking out the last few words of the sentence.

"Hello."

"Brian? Lionel, Cardiff."

Lionel Fanthorpe rarely uses his surname when identifying himself to his friends in outward calls, preferring his place of residence.

"Hi, Lionel," I said, attempting—unavailingly, of course—to match the cheerfulness and ebullience of his tone. "How's fame treating you?"

Lionel had recently achieved a measure of celebrity by virtue of being appointed the presenter of *Fortean TV*, a magazine program devoted to the not-entirely earnest investigation of weird events and individuals. This had caused a certain amount of controversy in the broadsheet press, some of whose columnists had thought it unbecoming of a minister of the Church of Wales to lend his dog-collar to such irreverence.

"It's marvelous," he assured me. "Actually, that's what I'm ringing about."

"You want me to appear on *Fortean TV*?" If I sounded skeptical, it's because I am—and it's because I'm universally renowned for my skepticism that I have every right to be skeptical about the possibility of ever being invited to appear on *Fortean TV*.

"Oh no, we're full up for the next series. It's just that ever since the first series I've been deluged with calls from all kinds of people clamoring to get on. You wouldn't believe some of the stories they tell."

"Actually, Lionel," I said, "I wouldn't believe any of the stories they tell—but I do believe that you've been deluged with calls. What do you expect if you set yourself up as the front man for rent-a-crank?"

"That's exactly why I thought you might be a valuable addition to our team," he told me, refusing to take the slightest offence. Lionel's geniality knows no bounds.

"You want me to be *Fortean TV*'s resident skeptic?"

"No, no. Forget *Fortean TV*. It's because Martin watched the show that he got in touch, but he doesn't want to be on it. He wants me to exorcise a supernatural presence in his bookshop."

If it had been anyone else on the other end of the line I'd have been perfectly certain that the word was "exercise", no matter how nonsensical the containing sentence might have become, but this was Lionel.

"Do you do exorcisms?" I asked.

"It's not something I do lightly," he assured me, "but if I'm convinced that it will do some good, I'm prepared to employ any of the Church's rituals. I believe that exorcism is a legitimate weapon in the war against evil." Lionel is what the Victorians would have described as a *muscular* Christian—not so much because he has a black belt in judo as because he believes that the power of active evil has to be countered by an equal and opposite reaction. He is the only man I know who could say "Praise the Lord and pass the ammunition!" with perfect sincerity.

"Why do you need me?" I said. "The presence of a strident atheist is hardly likely to help the party go with a bang. Assuming, of course, that departing demons do go with a bang, as well as the obligatory whiff of brimstone."

"I don't need you for the exorcism, even if there is one," said Lionel, cheerily. "I just thought you might be interested to sit in on a preliminary investigation—an all-night sitting—so that we can try to figure out exactly what we're dealing with. I read your thing in Steve's anthology."

"Ah," I said, as enlightenment dawned. Steve Jones had edited an anthology for Gollancz which consisted of famous

THE HAUNTED BOOKSHOP, BY BRIAN STABLEFORD

horror writers' true encounters with the supernatural. Not wishing to miss out on the opportunity I had supplied a piece entitled *"Chacun sa goule"* which offered a scrupulously accurate account of a real event: the coincidental discovery of a rare book by Maurice Maeterlinck, of whose existence I had been unaware until a few days earlier, at an antiquarian book fair I had stumbled across by chance. Typically, I had supplemented my record of the bare facts with a philosophical rhapsody about the existential significance of the continued permeation of the world by the carbonaceous matter that once made up the bodies of the dead. I had observed that the carbon dioxide in every breath we take contains atoms that might once have been part of the people of the past, whose minds also echo in the pages of their writings, so that the dead do indeed retain a "ghostly" presence in the present. Although graveyards were doubtless replete with such ghosts, I had said, the most significant of my own ghostly encounters invariably took place in bookshops. It was perhaps not unnatural, therefore, that on being told about a haunted bookshop—a bookshop whose resident supernatural presence was so discomfiting as perhaps to require exorcism—Lionel would think of me.

"Well?" said Lionel. "Are you interested?"

"What bookshop?" I parried. "Where?"

"It's a second-hand place—just down the coast, in Barry."

"There isn't a second-hand bookshop in Barry," I said, confidently. I once lived in Swansea for several years and I still visit my children there on occasion. If there had been a second-hand bookshop in Barry, I would have found mention of it in *drif's guide* and made the effort to visit it.

"It's not been there long," Lionel told me.

"And it's haunted already? Who by?"

"Martin's not sure that it's the premises. He thinks it might be the books."

I nearly came out with some crack about Martin presumably having picked up a copy of Abdul Alhazred's *Necronomicon* at a jumble sale in Tiger Bay but I hesitated. The idea of haunted books was not without a certain appeal—in fact, the mere mention of books was inevitably appealing to a man of my kind. Even the newest second-hand bookshop needs old books to dress its shelves. Most people anxious to move into the trade use their own collections as bases, but hardened collectors are usually so reluctant to put out their old favorites that they shop around for anything that can be bought in bulk at a reasonable price. I knew that there had been a time in the nineteenth century when the coal industry was booming and Cardiff was a busy port. The middle class had had aspirations in those days—C. D. Pamely's father had been a mining engineer in Pontypridd but he'd harbored greater ambitions for his sons—and it was possible that there were some nice caches of good antiquarian stock lurking in a place like Barry, which had been a haven for the south Wales gentry before slipping way down-market to become a third-rate holiday resort.

Haunted or not, there was just a slim possibility that the mysterious Martin's shop might have some interesting contents—and if it had opened too late to obtain an entry in the latest issue of *drif,* the professional vultures might not have had the chance to strip the shelves clean of tasty meat.

There is nothing that gladdens the heart of a book-collector like the thought of virgin stock. "It sounds interesting," I said to Lionel, effortlessly switching into earnest mode. "When do you propose to hold this investigative vigil?"

"Monday," said Lionel.

It was short notice, but I assumed that it would have been even shorter if Lionel hadn't been otherwise occupied on Sundays.

"Suits me," I said, firmly hooked and avid to be reeled in. "Name your time and place."

* * * * * * *

Lionel picked me up from Cardiff station in an old Cortina whose funereal paint job seemed appropriate to the occasion. He already had two passengers in place so I had no choice but to take a back seat. There wasn't a lot of space for me, let alone my overnight bag, but I squeezed myself in.

"This is Martin," Lionel said, indicating the middle-aged man whose claim to the front seat had obviously been secured by reason of dimension as well as opportunity, "and this is Penny, from the Society for Psychical Research."

"Is that still going?" I asked, nodding politely to a thin, thirty-ish woman with spectacles whose lenses were almost as powerful as mine. My relentlessly antiquarian mind inevitably associated the SPR with its late Victorian heyday, and the investigations of Katie King and D. D. Home mounted by the likes of William Crookes and Oliver Lodge. The woman seemed slightly resentful of my ignorance.

"Yes it is," she said, in a severe manner which suggested that she'd been warned about my skeptical tendencies—and also, perhaps, that she thought that taking a back seat to a man who presented *Fortean TV* was slumming it a bit.

"Penny's done postgrad research at Duke," said Lionel, proudly, as the car pulled way into the last remnants of the rush-hour traffic. "In the selfsame labs where J. B. Rhine once worked."

"I thought you could do that sort of thing in the UK now," I said. "Didn't Arthur Koestler leave a bequest to set up an established chair in paranormal studies? Somebody took the money in the end, didn't they?"

"There isn't a course here," the woman explained. "I wanted to do a proper course."

I didn't want to offend her further by challenging her use of the word "proper". Instead I cast an appraising eye over the equipment with which she had surrounded herself. I recognized the fancy temperature tracking-gauge and the video camera easily enough, but most of the rest was in leather cases, and it wasn't obvious what the ammeter on her knee was supposed to be connected to.

"Are we the whole squad?" I asked.

"For now," Lionel said. "If Penny gets anything interesting, she'll call in some of her associates for a more thorough investigation—with Martin's permission, of course." The way he added the qualifying clause made me wonder whether Martin's permissiveness might already have been severely tested by Lionel's insistence that a preliminary investigation would be necessary before deciding whether an exorcism might be required. I could understand why; even though the traditional silly season wouldn't be under way for another two months, the *Fortean Times* was hot enough nowadays to have all its best stories followed up by the *Sun* and the *Daily Star*, not to mention the *Sunday Sport*. That kind of coverage might boost the sales of a haunted bookshop for a week or two, but the embarrassment might last a lifetime.

"I hope the reverend explained to you, Mr. Stableford," the bookshop-proprietor intoned, in a broad way-up-the-valleys accent, "that this whole business is confidential."

"No one will hear a word of it from me," I assured him. "My lips are sealed." I can be very pedantic when giving out promises; while I type this page not a sound is escaping from my lips. I have not, of course, changed any of the names in the interests of protecting the innocent—or even the guilty—but you will doubtless have noticed that I have withheld the surnames of the minor characters.

"Perhaps you could fill Brian and Penny in while we're on the road, Martin," Lionel suggested. "Give them some idea of what to expect."

Martin did not seem overjoyed by this prospect. In fact, he looked as if he might be having second thoughts about the wisdom of having approached Lionel in the first place—but the incumbent at his local chapel was unlikely to do exorcisms, or to look kindly upon anyone who broached the possibility. The great majority of Welsh Methodists tend to the view that a man who imagines himself to be troubled by ghosts or demons is a man with an unusually guilty conscience, who should look deep into his own soul for the source of his disquiet.

"Would you rather I did it?" Lionel asked, his generosity as boundless as his geniality.

"No," said Martin, his mind quickly made up. "Best if...well, see, I'm from the Rhondda originally. In the industry till the pits closed—not a face worker, mind, always above ground. Middle management, I suppose, is the phrase they use nowadays. Anyhow, I was over twenty years in when the axe came down, an' the redundancy was a nice package. I'm only forty-three, so I knew I had to use the money—start a business, like. Well, I'd always been a reader, an' it just so happened that I was still in the office, tidying up, when one of the old boys we'd kept on to do the clearing up came in to ask what we wanted done with all the books from the old colliery library.

"I didn't even know there'd ever been a colliery library, but when the boys had found all these boxes of books in a storage-loft the old-timer had recognized them—said he'd often seen the like around his house in the old days, when his father and grandfather had been regular borrowers. It had fallen into disuse in the fifties, I suppose, what with paperbacks an' all, an' the room it was in had been turned into an office. So I said, it's all right, boys, I'll look after those—put what you can into my car, and pile the rest up in the bike-sheds. I'll ferry the boxes home a few at a time. Well, nobody else wanted them, did they?

"I thought at first I'd just look through them, like—sort out anything I wanted to read and give the rest to Oxfam—but when I got the old boy to help me stow the second batch he said that if I'd got a good home, he knew where the books from the old Workingmen's Institute had been put away when they turned it into a club an' the library was turfed out in favor of a snooker table. That's when I got the idea. Ours couldn't have been the only pit in Wales with its own library, nor our village the only one with a Workingmen's Institute, an' we're not the kind of folk to throw things away. Why not scout around, I thought, see what I could dig up, an' open a bookshop?"

Why not indeed? I thought, sympathetically.

"I knew there was no point doing something like that in the valley, mind," Martin continued, "or even in Merthyr. I thought of Caerleon first, but the wife wasn't happy about moving to what's practically England, an' I knew Cardiff already had two second-hand bookshops, so I thought of Barry, which the wife has always liked. It turned out that a lot of stuff from the old colliery libraries had been sold years ago to old Ralph in Swansea or that shop that used to be in the Hayes before it all got torn down, but I found four more sizeable lots that I picked up for next to nothing."

THE HAUNTED BOOKSHOP, BY BRIAN STABLEFORD

"How many books altogether?" I asked, impatient for hard news.

"About twelve thousand, give or take."

It wasn't as big a total as I'd hoped. Given the educational mission of nineteenth century Workingmen's Institutes, I guessed that at least half the books would probably be non-fiction and half the rest would probably be religious texts. Even if there were only three thousand volumes of fiction, however—and even if the bulk of those were standard sets of Scott and Dickens, there ought to be something of interest. None of the books had seen the light of day for at least twenty years, and some might not have been inspected for the best part of a century—and the most exciting fact of all was that Martin didn't seem to have a clue. In a business full of sharks, he was pure whitebait.

"How long, exactly, has the shop been open for business?" I asked.

"Open for business?" Martin echoed, incredulously. "It hasn't been open at all. Didn't the reverend...?"

"Sorry, Martin," Lionel interposed. "When I phoned Brian I didn't realize that you hadn't got that far."

My heart was still busy leaping. Not just virgin stock but extra virgin stock, untouched by sharkish fin!

"Do you think," Penny put in, resentfully, "that we could get to the paranormal activity?"

I had quite forgotten, in my excitement, that this was supposed to be a *haunted* bookshop. I remembered J. W. Dunne's theory that ghosts are images displaced in the fourth dimension from parallel worlds where time might be running ahead of or behind our own. If so, Martin's as-yet-unopened bookshop might easily be haunted by the shades of dozens of book dealers, all impatient to get into it.

"Yes," I said, trying to sound supportive of our collective mission. "Tell us about the ghosts."

"I never said *ghosts*," said Martin, his voice suddenly infected by a note of pedantic caution. "I never saw a *person*, you understand. Whatever it is, it's not people."

"Poltergeist phenomena, then?" said Penny, eagerly. "Books moving by themselves—pages turning. Or is it a matter of sudden chills, changes in atmosphere?"

THE HAUNTED BOOKSHOP, BY BRIAN STABLEFORD

"Bit of that, like," Martin conceded. "Wouldn't mind, if it were only that—cold, creaking an' so on."

"So what is it, exactly?" Penny wanted to know.

"Don't know, exactly. You're the expert, I suppose—you an' the reverend. I didn't notice anything at first—even the wife thought the place was all right, when it was empty. It's a lock-up, of course; we weren't planning on living there although it's got what the estate agent called living accommodation on the first floor. Modern family couldn't live there, even if their kids had long gone—too small by half, an' the bathroom facilities are woefully inadequate. I decided to use the so-called bedroom as a second stock-room, put shelves in an' everything. Plan was that when I'd got the shop going steady we'd both move down to a nice house overlooking the sea, but there's not much chance of that now until it's properly sorted—by the reverend, I mean. It's not so bad in daylight, of course, but even then...well, the wife's only been in there by day, an' she swears she'll never set foot in it again, even at high noon. I've been in there past midnight, putting up the shelves—but only the once, since I started putting out the stock. Seems as if the *presence* came with the stock, like, although it wasn't there when the books were all in boxes piled up in my hall an' front room. It's a real mystery."

"If it were a single haunted book," Lionel mused, "you might be able to solve the problem just by getting rid of that one volume."

"If it is," said Martin, darkly, "an' you can figure out which one, you can have it for nothing."

Given his account of how he'd acquired his stock, Martin could probably afford to be generous. Given that his stock had been on the shelves of private lending libraries for many years, though—and stored in various lofts and cupboards for many years more, without anyone complaining about any kind of haunting—it was difficult to see how the problem could be one of the books, or even all of them.

My preliminary judgment, inevitably, was that the problem was probably in Martin's mind. If he'd lived all his life in the Rhondda, heir to hundreds of years of mining tradition and having spent all his own working life in the industry, it must have been a terrible wrench to be forced to contemplate entry into an alien way of life. Reader or not, he was obviously no book-lover; he'd seen an opportunity and he'd felt obliged to seize it, but he must have thought himself caught between the devil of new endeavor and the deep blue sea of unemployment. Was it so very surprising that the devil in question had indeed turned, in his fearful mind, into a tangible force of darkness?

Lionel was still following his own train of thought. "What kind of book might that be, do you think?" he asked, of no one in particular. For a moment, I thought he was really going to bring up the *Necronomicon*, but he took the second worst option. "A grimoire, maybe? A copy of the *Key of Solomon*?"

"Sure," I said, sarcastically. "Every colliery in the valley used to have its resident wizard, who kept his secret lore on the top shelf of the library, bound up to look like records of coal-production. You shift sixteen tons, and what do you get? Another day older an' deeper in debt. Jesus don't you call me, 'cause I can't go—I owe my soul to the pithead whore." I was content to recite the words with only the faintest lilt; I have the singing voice of a crow with laryngitis.

"Actually," said Penny, "it wasn't unknown for eighteenth-century mines, and even for early factories, to have luckmen—wizards of a sort. Miners, especially, were very superstitious. It was a high-risk industry, you see. The transition from forced labor to wage-labor wasn't as long ago as you might think, even in these parts, and the transition from superficial workings—actual *pits*, that is—to deep shaft mining was a step into unknown territory. The activities of the luckmen would have been vital to the morale of their fellow-workers."

"Did they teach you that at Duke?" I asked, in a neutral tone.

"No," she said. "The LSE. I did a degree in sociology before I did my master's in parapsychology."

I'd been a lecturer in sociology at Reading for twelve years before I quit to write full-time, but I'd never heard of luckmen. On the other hand, I'd done my first degree in biology, so I'd never studied industrial sociology at all. "And were these luckmen in the habit of consulting books of protective rituals?" I asked.

"I don't know," she said.

"If they did," Lionel put in, "moving the book might have been the crucial disturbance—like moving bones laid to eternal rest. Didn't M. R. James once say that all his stories were variations on the theme of *curst be he who moves my bones*?"

"If it's a case of *curst be him who moves my books*," I opined, "we're more likely to be dealing with a dyed-in-the-wool book-collector than a black magician. I'd come back to haunt anyone who creased the dust-wrapper on one of mine. Hell hath no fury like a collector who finds a shopping-list scribbled on a flyleaf."

Lionel laughed, probably to be polite. Neither of the others cracked a smile. It looked as if it was going to be a long night, but I consoled myself with the knowledge that I could keep myself busy for hours with that much stock—fool that I was, I had no inkling of the horrible shock that was to come.

* * * * * * *

Martin's shop wasn't in a prime position, even by Barry's standards, but it was close enough to the seafront to catch a certain amount of passing trade during the holiday season. He was enough of a businessman to realize that his bread-and-butter business would be selling paperback pulp to people who needed something to occupy their eyes while they lay around on the beach, so the wooden shelves he'd erected in the window were stocked with best-sellers that looked as if they'd been culled from all the charity shops in south Wales.

When Martin unlocked the front door Penny and Lionel had enough respect for the alleged supernatural presence to pause for a moment, so I was first in. Although the sun hadn't quite set it was hidden by the houses on the far side of the street and the window display blocked out most of the light that was left, so I had to wait for Martin to switch on the electric light before I could actually set to work. It was not until the light came on that the full horror of the situation hit me.

I shouldn't have been surprised, of course, but rampant acquisitiveness generates the kind of optimism which allows inconvenient realizations to slip through the cracks of consciousness. One sweep of my gaze across the shelves on the back wall was sufficient to tell me what I should have guessed the moment Martin started going on about old colliery libraries and the innate reluctance of honest folk to throw anything away. Maybe if his name had been Hywel or Dai the awful datum would have clicked into place, but Martin was an English name. Alas, the books he'd picked up for "next to nothing"—the great majority of them, at least—were in Welsh.

What Martin had managed to acquire wasn't the entire stock of the old libraries, I realized, but merely that fraction of it that had been left behind when the readily-saleable stuff had gone—mostly texts whose utilitarian worth had been severely compromised by the fact that it was printed in a language falling swiftly into disuse.

If the bookshop really is haunted, I thought, bitterly, *the culprit is more likely to be a dead language than a dead man.*

"Do you get many Welsh speakers in Barry?" I asked, mournfully.

"Welsh is taught in all the schools," Martin said, proudly. "Legal requirement, see. Not so many speak it at home nowadays, of course, except up north—but people from Gwynedd go on holiday like anyone else. Can't keep a language alive without books, can you?"

By this time I had quick-scanned all eight of the shelves against the back wall and had turned my attention to the books behind the desk where the ancient cash-register stood. Most dealers keep their best stock—or what they think of as their best stock—behind their own station, to minimize the risk of theft. Not all the books behind the cash-register were in Welsh, but eighty per cent of them were, and the rest were evenly divided between books on mining and religious texts. This seemed to me to be a sad comment on Martin's values as well as his stock.

THE HAUNTED BOOKSHOP, BY BRIAN STABLEFORD

"Didn't the library stock include any English literature?" I asked him, plaintively. "Or any illustrated books, perhaps?"

"Some," Martin conceded. "I put the old fiction upstairs. That's standard practice, isn't it?" He'd obviously done a little market research and observed that most second-hand book dealers relegated the dross of ancient best-sellers and book club editions to the remotest corner they had. My spirits recovered a little; it was in such neglected corners that I always found my best bargains: rare works of nineteenth or early twentieth-century fantasy whose specialist significance was unappreciated by dealers whose own expertise was in railway books or natural history.

"The luckmen would have been Welsh speakers, of course," observed Penny, who was bringing in her second load of equipment and supplies while Lionel went back to the car for his third. "All their spells and incantations would have been handed down from time immemorial."

"They must have been true descendants of Merlin and Owen Glendower, mustn't they?" I put in, insouciantly. "The last custodians of the authentic Druidic tradition."

She looked at me as if I were a caterpillar in a salad sandwich. "Yes," she said, simply. "That's exactly what they were."

Diplomacy compelled me to refrain from making any clever remarks about Taliesin, the Bardic motto, Eisteddfods or male voice choirs. I eyed the rickety staircase that led up to the first floor, carpeted in what had once been red felt but was now almost completely black. "Is there a switch for the upstairs lights?" I asked Martin.

"There's one at the top on the left," he informed me, "and another just inside the door of the front room. You shouldn't need them, though—the windows up there let in more light than this one."

As I headed up the stairs I could feel renewed optimism putting a spring in my step. The uncluttered windows of the short corridor and the "so-called bedroom" did indeed let in more light than the window downstairs, but they were also a lot smaller, so the advantage was not as marked as I could have wished. Even so, I let the electric switch alone as I stepped through the open door into the room directly over the shop-front.

As soon as I had moved into the room the feeling hit me. It took me completely by surprise, and the impact was sufficient to make me catch my breath.

I had been in that room before.

I had, of course, experienced the commonplace sensation of *déjà-vu*, but never so intensely as to make me doubt the conventional explanation that it arises from an illusion generated when the same sensory information is accidentally duplicated in the brain, having been transmitted there by two distinct neuronal pathways. This was different, not just because of its intensity but because I knew—vaguely, at least—when and where I had had the experience that was being so carefully and so improbably reproduced by the present moment.

Most people, it is said, have recurring dreams. They may dream repeatedly of houses, of sexual encounters, of flying, or of appearing naked in public. When they have such dreams—or, at least, when they become conscious that they are having such dreams—they know that they are revisiting scenes already familiar: that the house is one they have previously visited in dreams, or that their power of flight is something that they are *re*discovering. Some such dreams may be enigmatic, perhaps because they are symbolically-disguised, but others are trivially literal; mine have always been perfectly understandable. My own recurrent dreams are of second-hand bookshops.

I have never considered it at all unusual that my long-standing addiction to combing the shelves of second-hand bookshops should be reflected in my dreams. Nor have I ever considered it unusual that such dreams should often be attended by the sense of returning to familiar haunts—because that, after all, is the form that the vast majority of my actual book-hunting trips take. It is only to be expected that when I dream of bookshops—or, at least, when I become conscious that I am dreaming of bookshops—I usually feel that they are familiar bookshops. Interestingly, however, they are never bookshops that really do exist in the everyday world; they are always imaginary bookshops. This means, of course,

THE HAUNTED BOOKSHOP, BY BRIAN STABLEFORD

that when I have the sense of having visited them before, I know that I can only have done so in other dreams. It is as if the virtual geography of my private dream-world numbers among its fixtures a series of shops, some fascinating and some not-so-fascinating, which I visit at irregular intervals: a population parallel to that with which the geography of the real world is dotted.

Sometimes, when dreaming of bookshops, I become conscious that I am dreaming—but I resist waking up, because I know that when I do I shall have to leave behind any interesting books I might have found. When my bookshop dreams become lucid in this fashion I often become conscious of the fact—or at least the illusion—that the shop I am in is one of which I have dreamed before.

Just as I had never dreamed of entering an actual bookshop, so I had never actually entered a bookshop of which I had dreamed. That I seemed to be doing so now was more than a cause for astonishment; it seemed, in fact, to be a violation of natural law, as threatening in its fashion as any conventional apparition or ominous shadow. I stood transfixed, appalled by the thought that I—a great and hitherto worthy champion of skepticism—could be assailed in this rude and nasty fashion.

Mercifully, the moment did not last. The shock of awful discovery was replaced soon enough by a struggle to remember what, if anything, I had found in this room when it had only been the figment of a dream. The mental reflex of the book-collector was powerful enough to drive away the alarm of revelation; I ceased to worry about the *how* of the mystery and focused my mind instead on the truly crucial question of what there might be to be found, and whether the illusion of having dreamed about the room—I was already content to dismiss the sensation as an illusion—might somehow assist my search.

No sooner had I begun to scan the nearest shelves, however, than the force of reality began to reassert itself upon my senses. The proportion of Welsh texts here was considerably less than on the shelves below—no more than half, and perhaps a little less—but that did not make the remainder seem significantly more promising. There were several sets of standard authors, more poetry than prose, in horribly shabby pocket editions. My expert eye immediately picked out a number of yellowbacks, but their condition was so awful that it would hardly have mattered had they been more interesting titles than they were. A few bound volumes of old periodicals turned out on closer inspection to be *Sunday at Home* and *Pick-Me-Up*, not even *Longman's* or *Temple Bar*, let alone anything more interesting.

In brief, it looked like the kind of stock over which a collector might toil for hours in order to turn up a couple of items whose significance to his collection was marginal at best. Not, of course, that I could contentedly let it alone; I knew that I would indeed have to inspect every single shelf. lifting every volume whose title was not clearly inscribed on its spine, in order to make perfectly certain that nothing evaded me. No matter how laborious the task became, I would have to stick to it come hell or high water—but first I had to return downstairs, in answer to Lionel's urgent call.

* * * * * * *

All Lionel wanted, it turned out, was to hand me a cup of tea and ask my opinion as to what kind of pizza he ought to have delivered.

There is nothing like a four-way debate about pizza toppings to bring a ghost-hunting expedition right down to earth; by the time we had settled on two mediums, one with bacon, mushroom and tomato and the other with olives, anchovies and pepperoni, mundanity had such a secure hold on Martin's bookshop that even Madame Arcati at her most lunatic would have been hard-pressed to find the least hint of spirit activity.

By this time, of course, Penny and Lionel had set up all the SPR's apparatus. The video camera was on its tripod, ready to be spun around in quest of the kinds of things that one glimpses in the corners of one's eyes. A quaint little pointer was inscribing a record of the room's temperature on a slowly-rotating drum. (I was glad to note that since we had entered the shop our combined body-heat had contrived to raise the temperature by a whole degree Celsius to a reasonably comfortable sixteen.) I still wasn't sure what it was that the ammeter was hooked up to but whatever it was had not yet succeeded in generating a flicker of current.

Lionel asked Penny to tell him a little more about luckmen and their role in the mines of yore, but Penny had already run to the limit of her information on the subject so she tried to pump Martin about residual superstitions in the modern industry—a subject on which he was not at all forthcoming.

"I was always above ground, see," he said. "The boys at the face had their own little community—they'd tell you tales for a laugh, like, but they'd never let on that they took any of it seriously."

"What tales?" Lionel wanted to know.

"*You* know. Not a pit in the valley has a clean sheet mortality-wise—not any that's been open longer than twenty years, anyhow. The oldest are full of worked-out shafts and old rock falls, an' there's always talk of voices—voices of men killed by gas or crushed, you see. Offering warnings as often as not; I've heard far more tales of men being saved than men being lost. Nobody goes down a pit needs scaring, see; work's dangerous enough without that."

"Judging by the dust on some of the books upstairs," I said, "one or two of them must have made a good number of trips down into the shafts."

"I doubt that," Martin said. "No time to read down there, nor light good enough to read by. The dust on the bindings is the kind that gets in everywhere—the fine stuff that hangs about in the air and never quite washes out. Almost like a liquid, it is, or a *miasma*—smears and clings and blackens even if you never set foot in the cage or a hand on a hopper."

I had to admire the way he pronounced "miasma", lingering over the vowels as only a Welshman could.

"The dark spirit of the pit," said Penny, softly. It would almost have been enough to make us look over our shoulders if we hadn't heard the delivery boy's moped rattling over the potholes in the street. We fell upon the pizza-slices with the kind of eager rapacity that only competition can generate, even though we all knew perfectly well that we were only entitled to four apiece.

THE HAUNTED BOOKSHOP, BY BRIAN STABLEFORD

While we ate, darkness fell—and shadows crept upon us in spite of the electric light. Martin, born and bred to the economy of the valleys, had only fitted sixty-watt bulbs.

Martin was watching us now, alert for any sign of tension or unease. As with many Celts, his eyes were pale even though his hair was dark, but they weren't blue; they were as grey as slate. Although Penny was a very different physical type—ectomorphic rather than endomorphic—she had very similar coloring. Her eyes did retain a slight hint of blue but her complexion lacked the hint of rosy pink that Martin's had. Lionel must have been at least twenty years older than Martin and thirty years older than Penny but he looked more robust than either of them. He was originally from Norfolk, which probably meant that he—like me—was a descendant of Viking settlers. *Our* ancestors had never been bards or druids; our family trees were as devoid of luckmen as of mistletoe.

I was prepared to feel a slight pang of regret about that; I knew that if I were going to find any real treasure in that dust-caked morass upstairs I was going to need some luck. Even while we ate my restless eyes were checking and rechecking the downstairs shelves, unable to find anything worth lingering over.

The pizza was as mediocre as could be expected, but the tea was better. It seemed much better until I got to the dregs, when I began to notice an odd aftertaste. I noticed, too, that the air in the shop had a peculiar texture to it. All bookshops are dusty, of course, and when books that have been a long time in storage are first set on shelves they often release a little dampness into the air, faintly polluted with fungal spores and bits of dead silverfish. Book-lovers learn to savor that kind of atmosphere, or at least to ignore it—but this texture was slightly different from any I'd encountered before. This gave the impression of being vintage dust—a real *grand cru*. Martin's pronunciation of the word "miasma" echoed in my mind as I tried to measure the dust's quality more precisely, but it didn't seem dismissable simply as coal dust any more than it warranted elevation to the status of "the dark spirit of the pit". It was something more teasing than either.

The Haunted Bookshop, by Brian Stableford

I couldn't help thinking of the skeptical kind of occult detective stories, where the intrepid investigators eventually find that alleged hauntings are merely noxious vapors released from bad drains or unusual chemical reactions. Was it possible, I wondered, that the redistribution of books kept so long in close confinement really had set free some disturbing vapor that had been patiently building up in the inner recesses of the boxes for decades? I didn't like to suggest to the others that perhaps we should have brought a canary.

"Well," I said, as soon as I had bolted my last allotted slice of bacon, mushroom and tomato. "I'm going to get started on the upstairs stock. If you need me, just scream."

"Will you be all right up there on your own?" Martin asked, as if he sincerely believed that I might not be.

"If I'm not," I assured him, "*I'll* scream."

"If you find any of mine," said Lionel, "let me know." Long before he got religion Lionel was the most prolific writer of science fiction and supernatural fiction in Britain, producing over a hundred and eighty volumes for the late unlamented Badger Books at the princely sum of £22 10s a time. His one long-running series had consisted of occult detective stories starring the redoubtable Val Stearman and his lovely female associate La Noire. Stearman had, of course, been modeled on the young Lionel, and his spirit was doubtless still active even though the containing flesh had suffered a little. It required an extremely optimistic eye, alas, to find the slightest hint of La Noire in Penny-from-the-SPR.

"I will," I promised.

* * * * * * *

This time, I had to use the electric lights. I made a mental note to bring my own hundred-watt bulbs if I ever got involved in a similar vigil in future. I started my search in the top left-hand corner of the shelf-unit to the left of the door and began to work methodically across and down, across and down.

If you've ever browsed the less popular shelves in the London Library you'll know how dust from the red leather bindings that are gradually rotting down will stain your hands and your shirt, so that a long session in French Fiction can leave you looking suspiciously like Jack the Ripper. Exploring these shelves was not dissimilar, but it was an order of magnitude worse. Within ten minutes my hands were absolutely filthy, and my green corduroy jacket was beginning to turn black. My shirt and my jeans had started out black but that didn't spare them any manifest effect, because the dust was so fine as to be *slick* and it soon made itself felt in their texture. If the dust had been pure carbon it would, I suppose, have been graphite, but even the best Welsh anthracite isn't anywhere near pure carbon. This was *impure* carbon, and its impurities were enhancing its ability to form a *miasma*.

I couldn't help wiping my hands periodically on my jeans, even though I knew that it wasn't helping the situation. Nor could I help occasionally touching my hand to my face, my forehead and my hair, even though I knew that such touches would leave smudges. By the time I'd done twenty feet of shelves—without finding a single book that I'd have been happy to pay more than 50p for—I knew that I must be a real sight, and what Martin had said about the woeful inadequacy of the bathroom facilities suddenly began to seem more relevant.

Despite the aforementioned inadequacy, my companions stumped up the staircase one by one to use the facilities. Lionel was the only one who looked in to see how I was doing. When I stopped for a break myself I took the opportunity to inspect my features in the mirror, and I managed to scrub off the worst of the stains with toilet paper, but even a thorough soaping failed to shift the worst of the grime from my fingers.

As I resumed my labors I remembered what I'd written in *'Chacun sa goule'* about our breathing in the carbon dioxide relics of the dead every time we fill our lungs. To the extent that the dust-particles on the books were coal they were presumably the relics of creatures that had roamed the earth in the Carboniferous Era: the flesh of early dinosaurs compounded with the mass of gymnosperm tree-trunks and the chitin of giant insects. That ancient carbon must, however, be mingled with echoes of more recent lives and deaths: the lives and deaths of the men who hewed the coal, or that minority among them who had tried, valiantly, to improve their minds with the aid of the written word.

Once, at the University of Reading, I had attended an open lecture in which A. N. Wilson had argued that the rich inner life of thought and feeling, which we now take completely for granted, is largely a product of books, and most especially of novels. Men who lived and died confined by oral culture, Wilson argued, had not the mental resources to build a robust inner monologue, a pressurized stream of consciousness. If that were true, I thought, such men could hardly be in any position to leave ghosts behind when they died and decayed. If dust really could retain some kind of spirit, it would, of necessity, be the spirit of *readers*—in which case, book-dust ought to be the most enspirited of all.

As I formed that strange thought, the sensation of having been in that room before returned in full force, swiftly and irresistibly.

I did not pause in my routine of plucking the books off the shelves, inspecting their title-pages and returning them, but the automatism of that routine suddenly became oppressive and seemingly unnatural. Before, when the sensation had come over me, I had thought it an anomaly: a sensation that I should only have been capable of feeling in a dream— but now it did not feel anomalous at all, because it seemed now that I really was *in a dream*, where I was perfectly entitled to remember bookshops visited in other dreams, and to dwell in the curious nostalgia of discoveries barely made before being lost in the moment of awakening. As in all such episodes of lucidity, I had not the slightest desire to wake; indeed, I had the strongest possible desire to remain as I was, potentially able to grasp and hold any treasure that wishful thinking might deliver into my horrid night-black hand.

The light of the sixty-watt bulb grew dimmer, and the walls of the room drew closer. The spines of the books grew darker, and the air became thicker and heavier. Because I knew that I was in a dream-state, I wasn't unduly worried— to the contrary, I was intent on preserving a state in which the power of desire might be adequate to lead me to a precious find. It occurred to me that the room had become uncannily like a pit, both literally and metaphorically. The dross on the shelves was the stone of the imagination, inert and useless, while the texts for which I was searching were pregnant with mental energy that only needed to be read in order to warm and illuminate my inner being.

Because I already possess twenty thousand volumes my want list has been shrinking for years, and the works that I yearn most desperately to find nowadays are so rare that it would require a veritable miracle of luck to locate affordable copies. Without any magical ritual to aid me in my search through Martin's stock I had only honest toil to bring to my task: a simple, straightforward determination to make certain that nothing would escape my notice. I searched with relentless efficiency. I worked methodically along the shelves, ignoring the miasmic dust, in the frail hope that somewhere beneath its obscuring cloak a treasure trove might be waiting: a copy of *Gyphantia*, or *Omegarus and Syderia*, or *The Mummy!*, or *The Old Maid's Talisman*, in any edition and any condition, provided only that the text were complete.

It soon became so difficult to draw breath that I felt slightly dizzy, and so dark that I had no alternative but to pause in my work. I was already kneeling down, inspecting the lowest shelf in a unit, but I had to put out a hand nevertheless to support myself against the shelves. My eyes began to play tricks on me; phosphenes lit up the black air like a cluster of stars, and the darkness itself began to flow and shift, as if it were alive with a host of bustling shadows: a host so vast and so crowded that its individual parts were jostling for presence in a narrow corridor that was growing narrower by the instant.

The dust that lay upon the air now seemed so dense that the air was indeed *liquid*. My trachea closed reflexively and I found myself gulping, swallowing the air and the intoxicating spirit which possessed and saturated it.

I was not afraid. I was secure in my conviction that an instant of panic would be enough to bring me out of the dream-state and back to wakefulness, and I had dreamed far too many dreams of this frail kind to allow panic its moment of opportunity. I drank the spirits of the dead, and drank them gladly. I drank them thirstily, because I knew that they were closer to me than any mere kin. What was my own spirit, after all, but a compound of all that I had read and inwardly digested? Even if A. N. Wilson were mistaken in his estimate of the majority of men, he was surely right about himself and he was right about me. *My* inner life, *my* pressurized stream of consciousness, was the product of texts and the love of texts. I had been a ghoul all my life; what had I to be afraid of in that dark room full of clamorous spirits? The greater part of my life, and the greater part of my emotion, had been spent and generated by intercourse with the dead; what need had I to feel threatened, or to suspect the presence of maleficent evil?

I drank deeply, avid for further intoxication. The dust was, after all, a previously-untasted vintage.

I felt slightly stirred, as if moist wind and cloying warmth were washing over me but leaving no impression. I felt the fading gleam of the Celtic twilight in my lungs and in my heart. I felt the heritage of Merlin and Taliesin and the force of Druid magic in my brain and in my groin. I heard the musical voices of luckmen intoning their spells, mingled with the strangled cries of hewers choked by gas or crushed by falling stone, all echoing together in the empty spaces of my mind.

It was a delicious fantasy, a haunting dream: a fantasy so delicious and a dream so haunting that I would dearly have liked to maintain it against the cruel penetration of lucidity—but I could not do it.

My supporting hand moved along the wooden shelf and my senses reeled. It was only the slightest of adjustments but the little finger picked a thin splinter out of the distressed wood, and the tiny stab of pain made me gasp. The gasp turned to a cough, and then to a fit of coughing—and a cataract of black dust cascaded out of my mouth into the palm of my hand.

The sixty-watt bulb buzzed and flickered, and its light became noticeably brighter. I hauled myself to my feet, blinked away the moment of drowsiness, and went to the bathroom to rinse my hands again. Having done that, as best I could, I went back to the place at which I had paused and started scanning the top shelf of the next unit.

THE HAUNTED BOOKSHOP, BY BRIAN STABLEFORD

I didn't curse myself for losing the dream. Dreams are by nature fragile and fugitive, and only death can free us, in the end, from the everpresent duty of waking from their toils.

****

It took me a further three-quarters of an hour to finish searching the upstairs room. The best items I found were a couple of bound volumes of *Reynolds' Miscellany*, including the serial version of Reynolds' *Faust* and battered copies of Eugène Sue's *Martin the Foundling*, George Griffith's *A Criminal Croesus*, and Mrs.. Riddell's *Fairy Water*. They were all in poor condition, but they were all titles that I'd be glad to add to my collection. Considering that the hunt had started so unpromisingly it didn't seem to be a bad haul, and there was still a slight possibility that I could add to it from the ground floor stock.

Lionel, Martin, and Penny were sitting downstairs, all as quiet as church mice. I thought at first that they might be asleep, and I took care to tiptoe down the last few steps, but Lionel looked around and said: "There's more tea in the pot. We've all had a second cup." His voice was slower than usual and a little thicker.

"I'm okay," I assured him. "Seen any sign of *the presence*?"

"Not *seen*, exactly," he told me, "but we definitely felt something, didn't we?"

"It's not as bad as it has been," Martin said, evidently disgruntled by the failure of his shop to come up with the goods, "but I can feel it."

"How about you?" I said to Penny.

"Nothing objective," she said, looking sadly at her various instruments. "But I can feel *something*. It's faint, but it's there." I could tell from the tone of her voice that she was disappointed. It's hard to impress people with subjective feelings; she knew that unless she could carry away some kind of tangible record—a clip of film, a trace on her rotating chart or a leaping needle on the ammeter—she'd have nothing to interest the punctilious inquisitors of the Society for Psychical Research.

THE HAUNTED BOOKSHOP, BY BRIAN STABLEFORD

"Anything upstairs?" Lionel asked, obviously expecting a negative answer.

"Just books," I said. "Hundreds and hundreds that no one will ever want to read—and a few dozen that someone might. I've only found a few, but they won't just sit on my shelves unread. I feel sorry for the rest, in a way. All that thought that went into their creation! All that effort! If they only had voices, they'd be clamoring for attention, don't you think? They'd be excited, wouldn't they, at having been taken out of their coffins at last and put on display? They probably thought that the Day of Judgment had come at last when Martin first unpacked them—but disillusionment must be setting in by now. How long do you think it takes a book to give in to despair? Not long, I expect, if it's a book from a colliery library—a book that has already had a taste of the darkness of the abyss."

"You're not taking this seriously, are you?" Martin said, without undue rancor. "It's all a joke to you."

"The trouble with skeptics," Penny added, taking care to couch her remarks in general terms, "is that they're too enthusiastic to accept their own insensitivity as proof that there's nothing to be sensitive to. They're like blind men denying that sight is possible. Not everyone's the same, you know. Everybody's different, and some of us can feel the presence of things that others can't."

"Perhaps you're right," I said, mildly. "You don't mind if I move about, do you? I'll try not to disturb you."

"Feel free," said Lionel, with typical *bonhomie*. "There's no need for us to sit still or be quiet. There's a long night still ahead of us—plenty of time for the presence to make itself felt more keenly, if it cares to."

He was absolutely right, of course—the night that stretched before us was very long indeed. I did my bit, and never closed my eyes for a moment. Once I'd finished checking the downstairs stock I perched on a wooden chair and chatted to Lionel about anything and everything except religion. We remembered a few old times and a few old friends; he told me all about *Fortean TV* and I told him about all the stories and article I'd written lately. I expect the others found it more than a little boring, although Lionel kept bringing them into the conversation at every possible opportunity. He likes to be the life and soul of every party, and he sometimes succeeds in that, even when it seems to be an uphill struggle. He was the commanding presence in the bookshop now; his was the personality which filled it.

All the while, I watched the three of them. I watched them watching, waiting for something that always seemed to be on the brink of arriving but never quite did. They did feel another, darker presence—of that I was sure, although they made no elaborate attempt to describe or discuss it—but they had no idea what it was. They wanted it to become more clamorous, not so much because that would reveal it more fully and more clearly, but because they thought that the clamor might somehow contain its own explanation—but it never did. Its brief hold on the atmosphere of the shop was loosening; it needed no exorcism to persuade it to slip away into oblivion. Hour by hour and inch by inch, Martin's haunted bookshop became *dispirited*.

So far as I could tell, we did nothing to encourage the slow decay of the presence, but we did nothing to prevent it. None of us had the least idea how to encourage it, and none of us would have wanted to had we known how.

As the time passed I watched my three companions become sleepier and sleepier as habit tested their resolve. I heard their voices slow and slur as dreams reached out for them even while they struggled to stay awake—but wakefulness won the war, and the dreams that might have claimed them had they been alone evaporated into the increasingly empty air. The dust stirred up by Martin's exertions was already beginning to settle out and to settle down, adsorbed on to the surfaces of wall and window, carpet and ceiling. Even when I first sat down the air was no longer vintage air; as the morning progressed it became flatter and more insipid, increasingly soured by the faint odors of living flesh.

By the time dawn broke, Martin and Penny were agreed that the presence had gone—that its hold was broken. Martin was slightly anxious that it might return as soon as it could find him on his own again, but Lionel assured him that he would be more than willing to come back if Martin thought it necessary, and would be happy to spend the night alone on the premises if that was the only way to bring the presence out. The way he said it told me that he didn't expect any such thing to occur; without quite knowing how he knew it, he was convinced that the presence had loosened its grip and lost its hold.

We had breakfast in a café before starting back to Cardiff. Lionel drank lots of black coffee to make sure that he was in no danger of falling asleep at the wheel, although he was no stranger to all-night vigils. In the event, we got back to the railway station without the least hint of alarm.

"You didn't have a wasted journey, anyhow," Lionel said, as I got out of the car. He was looking at my overnight bag, which was bulging with the books I'd bought at a pound apiece—a perfectly reasonable price, considering that they were only reading copies—from the parsimonious Martin.

"Not in the least," I said. "To tell you the truth, I don't think any of us did. Sometimes, all it takes to exorcise a presence is to fill a place with people and talk of ordinary matters. Perhaps Martin will feel more at home in the shop from now on."

"Let's hope so," said Lionel. "Thanks for coming down."

I waved goodbye as the car pulled away. I slept on the train, dreamlessly, all the way back to Reading.

When I got up to leave the train I noticed that the orange upholstery was stained with black. I knew that my jacket would have to go to the dry-cleaners and my jeans into the washing-machine, but I had every faith in the ability of modern technology to clear away the last residues of the dust. Ours is an inhospitable world for matter out of place and mind out of time

* * * * * * *

Lionel called me a week later to say that Martin had had no further trouble with paranormal phenomena and discomfiting presences, but that he'd decided to get rid of the shop anyway.

"He reckons that he's not cut out to be a book dealer," Lionel informed me, sadly. "He says there's a world of difference between being a reader and being a real bookman, and that he's obviously just a reader. He thinks he might look for a little newsagent's shop, or a pizza franchise."

"Good luck to him," I said.

"Penny's gone up to Scotland to investigate an old mansion. It's only the Lowlands, she says, but it's still more promising ground than Barry. The Scots are more firmly rooted in their native soil, she says. They're more closely in touch with their ancestors, and they're far too wise to doubt the nearness of the Other World."

"Good luck to her, too," I said. "How about you?"

"Still skating on that thin crust called reality," he assured me, quoting the catch-phrase he uses in every episode of *Fortean TV*. "You won't believe some of the stuff we've got lined up for the next series. Be sure to watch it, won't you?"

"Actually, Lionel," I told him, "I won't believe any of it. But I'll tune in religiously just the same."

THE HAUNTED BOOKSHOP, BY BRIAN STABLEFORD

BEYOND BLISS

I was working on a story called "The Bookworms" when Lionel Fanthorpe called me from Cardiff to ask me if I wanted to take part in an experiment.

"What sort of experiment?" I asked. As a minister in the Church of Wales and the presenter of *Fortean TV*, Lionel has fingers in a lot of pies, very few of which are the run-of-the-mill steak-and-kidney variety.

"It's all above board," he assured me. "The people in charge have doctorates from respectable universities, and they're based at the University of Glamorgan."

The University of Glamorgan had once refused even to interview me for a job teaching creative writing, and they're the only university in the UK to offer a degree in science fiction, so I didn't find this news at all reassuring. "Yes, Lionel," I said, patiently, "but what is the experiment supposed to prove? And what does it actually entail?" My one invariable principle regarding experiments is that if there are needles involved, I'm not.

"They're trying to get in touch with the Cosmic Mind," he said, blandly. "No drugs. Just light hypnosis, a little suggestion—and music."

"I'm the world's worst hypnotic subject," I told him. "My mother was a hypnotherapist for many years before she retired to Spain, and she'll give me a reference if you ask her. Mind like a stone wall. Suggestibility, on any scale you care to name, less than absolute zero."

"I know," he said. "That's why we want you. Axel and Claire asked me to recommend the most skeptical person I'd ever met, and yours was the first name that came to mind. They need someone who not only doesn't believe in the

69

Cosmic Mind but would continue to disbelieve in it even if he were staring it in the face...or in touch with it even more intimately than that."

Like the next man, I can resist anything except flattery. Or temptation. Or torture. Or...well, that's not the point.

"You want me to be some sort of control sample?" I said, while I thought it over.

"Exactly," he said. "If they only do the experiment with believers, you see, there's a danger that no one will take them seriously. It's difficult to get this kind of work through any kind of peer review."

"I didn't know *The Fortean Times* used a peer review system," I said. "Although I suppose it's the only journal in the world that could run its articles past Sir Isaac Newton, Mothman, and Beelzebub. If the Cosmic Mind signs up for the team, though, I suppose you can dispense with the small fry."

"Very funny," said Lionel. "Are you interested or not? They'll pay your train fare to Pontypridd and back for the preliminary investigation, plus overnight accommodation and a fifty pound fee. It's not much, I know, but...."

"But if it works I get to chat with the Cosmic Mind. Who knows what we might have in common? I hope he doesn't want me to put him in a book, though—I'm a serious skiffy writer. Did I say *he?* I meant *she*, of course. Or *it*. Or...."

"Is Friday all right?" Lionel asked, interrupting the joke in his customary cavalier fashion, generously covering up the fact that I hadn't actually thought of a punch line. "About one o'clock. We'll meet you at the station."

"Okay," I said. "I wouldn't do it for anyone else, mind—I'm a busy man. I'm working on a story in which a high-minded genetic engineer named Bowdler manufactures a new kind of worm that eats and excretes ink, with a view to training it to substitute sets of asterisks for expletives. When he's successful, though, other interested parties are quick to move in. The Iranian mullahs start mass producing a subspecies that can convert every text in the world into the *Quran*, forcing the scientific community to close ranks and produce a host of antidote species to reverse the process. Then, of course, natural selection kicks in, and the struggle for intellectual hegemony begins in earnest. The *Quran*-producers soon fall by the wayside because they're unable to adapt, but the ones that colonize the Bible-munching niche soon evolve to the point at which everything from *Genesis* to *Revelation* is converted into trails of excreta representing the complete works of Voltaire, David Hume, and Richard Dawkins—which, of course, forces all the Biblical fundamentalists to start singing from a new hymn-sheet. After that...well, I don't want to give away the ending. It might to sell to *Analog*—especially if I take Voltaire out and put Robert A. Heinlein in."

"But you'll have to bring your own music," Lionel added, as if he hadn't been listening—although he was almost certainly running a bluff while he calculated the chances of nicking my plot and getting the story written before I could finish it.

"Music?" I said. "What music?"

"Your favorite music. It's an accessory to the hypnotic process—part of the method. Trance and dance equals transcendence."

"I don't dance," I told him, frostily. The equation sounded vaguely familiar, but it was more Russell Hoban than Deepak Chopra, so I wasn't entirely unsympathetic. I don't mind life imitating art, so long as it shows a modicum of good taste.

"No, of course not. You can't actually dance while you're hooked up to the equipment. Not physically. It's more like dancing *inside*. Within the trancing, that is."

I didn't waste any time imaginatively pursuing possible puns on the word trancing, that being the kind of thing best left to the managers of boy bands.

"My favorite music's Goth rock," I told him. "I think the TM brigade prefer Hindu chants to Fields of the Nephilim."

"Bring along a few CDs," Lionel said. "Five or six should be enough. See you Friday."

"Okay," I said. "Tell the Cosmic Mind to expect me, and not to be too intimidated by my reputation."

* * * * * * *

THE HAUNTED BOOKSHOP, BY BRIAN STABLEFORD

I hesitated over the new Fields of the Nephilim CD, but decided in the end to go for the classics and picked out *Elizium* and *Revelations*. To show willing, I also packed Ataraxia's *Lost Atlantis*, the Garden of Delight's *Necromanteion IV* and Sopor Aeternus and the Ensemble of Shadows' *Dead Lovers' Sarabande*. I figured that if they couldn't get me in the mood for a chat with the Cosmic Mind, nothing would.

The train journey wasn't too bad, except for the connection that went from Cardiff to Pontypridd. I spent the time productively, reading Villiers de l'Isle Adam's *Tribulat Bonhomet*. It isn't easy to read French texts without a dictionary, but making up English equivalents for all the French words you don't know is always a stimulating exercise, and you can revel in the faint but exciting possibility that the text you've part-improvised might actually be an improvement on the original. Then again, it's a lot better for the image than reading *Viz*.

Lionel was waiting to meet me, as promised, with two companions. Actually, they'd turned up fifteen minutes late, but so had the train. I find that life is replete with such wonderful coincidences, even when I'm not slightly late for an appointment with the Cosmic Mind; I expect that everyone else does too.

"This is Claire Louchon," said Lionel, introducing the taller of his two companions. "And this is Axel Castle." I had a brief flash of *déjà-vu* as I remembered the two psychic researchers Lionel had had in tow when he invited me along to see his so-called haunted bookshop a couple of years before, although these two didn't look a day over twenty-one in spite of the fact that they were pretending as hard as they could to be serious scientists. Axel even had a tweed jacket that wouldn't button up over his beer belly, and Claire had glasses with blue-tinted lenses the size of coasters.

"Hi," I said. "How's the getting-in-touch business going? Anyone been turned into a gibbering wreck by the sheer Lovecraftian cosmic horror of realizing man's absolute insignificance within the unutterable bleakness of the universe?"

THE HAUNTED BOOKSHOP, BY BRIAN STABLEFORD

"We can't discuss the other experimental runs," Claire said, as the four of us clambered into a dark blue Hyundai. "There's a danger of prejudicing your expectations." She had got into the driver's seat, so I assumed that it was her car. Lionel got into the front passenger seat, so I was left to share the back with Axel.

"Fair enough," I said. "I take it that we are observing the principle of informed consent, though. You have to tell me what you're actually going to do to me, even if you don't go into details about the theory."

"Oh, we don't mind telling you a little bit about the theory," Axel said, once we were all belted up. "And the experimental design is quite simple, although the equipment does look a trifle intimidating. We couldn't afford a full-scale sensory deprivation tank, so it's just a comfy chair in a bare room, really. You'll have headphones, of course, to play the hypnostream and the music, but we'll tape two halves of a ping pong ball over your eyes to cut out visual stimuli. We'll put an electrode net over your skull, but it'll feel just like a hairnet—nothing heavy."

"Hypnostream?" I queried.

"That's what we call the relaxation tape. Lionel tells me that your mother's a hypnotherapist, so you must have heard dozens of them. We'll play that for an hour or so until the EEG tells us you're ready; then we'll add in the music, very discreetly. We don't play it loudly, of course—just above the threshold of audibility. There's one further phase, but it's not invasive and it's perfectly harmless."

"I don't relax," I warned him. "Mind like a steel blade."

"You sleep, don't you?" was Axel's mild reply. "Your brain knows how to navigate through all the phases of semi-consciousness, even if your mind refuses to take notice."

"I never remember my dreams. If you put me to sleep, I won't remember a thing when I wake up."

"That's a possibility. We're not aiming for sleep, though. Have you ever done any meditation?"

"No. Mostly, I let my endorphins do their own thing. I figure that if I start inducing bliss states on a daily basis I might get addicted. A writer needs his presence of mind around the clock—clarity of mind too, if he can manage it, although I will admit that there are plenty of bestsellers who've never even got close."

"That's good," he said, amiably. "We're certainly not aiming for a bliss state—or, for that matter, a conventional restful alert state—any more than we're aiming for everyday sleep. We're trying to reach much more deeply into the primitive parts of the mind than standard meditation techniques, perhaps even deeper than the bliss state that experienced meditators claim to be able to reach."

The landscape we were driving through still bore the scars of a thousand years of mining, but none of the pits was active any more and the slag-heaps were slowly being reclaimed by heroic weeds. Whatever coal was still beneath us was distributed in all manner of inconvenient seams, whose exploitation was no longer economic. The pits could have gone deeper, but it wasn't worth the trouble—not, at least, until the gas ran out. For the time being, the people of the valleys had to scrape a living on the surface, where everything was dingy green and slate grey instead of honest pitch-black.

"Sounds great," I told Axel, who seemed to be waiting for a reply. "Reverse all the way from the cerebrum into the hind-brain, turn left at the hypothalamus and drive a mineshift straight down the spinal cord to oblivion. Unravel four billion years of mental evolution, chuck the mental strata of civilization, animality, and vegetation on the nearest slag-heap, follow the dark seam until it peters out into the gaseous flow and fizz of the ultraconsciousness of cyanobacterial slime. Trance and dance equal spiritual strip-tease."

"Very neat, Dr. Stableford. Are you, by any chance familiar with the thesis that the brain, rather than generating consciousness, actually restricts it?"

"Sure," I said. It takes more than a twenty-something psychologist from the University of Glamorgan to wrongfoot me. "One version of Cosmic Mind theory derives from Lamarckian and Bergsonian evolutionary theory, suggesting that the sentience of the universe permeates everything by providing us with a kind of elementary teleological impulse. Primitive organisms, in this view, aren't individually conscious, but they participate in some infinitesimally small way in the vast motion of a universal train of thought. As they become more advanced, though, the brain evolves to isolate the individual from the cosmic mindstream, enclosing and usurping a little of its potential, which can be organized and formulated as a *self*...eventually, when brains become as skilful as human brains, into a self-conscious self, which naturally comes to the conclusion that it's independent and self-contained—perhaps even alone, if it's solipsistically inclined—even though it's only the feeblest echo of that from which it has been incompletely extracted. Although ignorant of its true nature and origin, it nevertheless retains an intuition of the Whole and cannot help yearning for reconnection, even though the price of that reconnection would be the effective annihilation of the individual.

"If it only had the evolutionist input to sustain it, the theory would have petered out like the Welsh mining industry, but the notion has been rebooted by physicists hung up on the uncertainty principle. If observers are required to collapse wave-functions and bring concrete events out of the hesitant fuzz of subatomic potentiality, the universe must have required an observing consciousness long before we—or the cyanobacteria—first evolved. In this way of thinking, some form if Universal Consciousness is an elementary condition of existence. So quantum mechanics now plays deism to *élan vital*'s theism. Whatever next, eh?"

"That's very good," said Axel.

"No it isn't," said Claire, cool as a cucumber behind her blue shades. "It's contemptuous, oversimplified crap, which doesn't begin to do justice to the notion of the implicate order, the quantum-computer theory of intelligence or the essential paradoxicality of voluntarism. You don't need to humor this one, Axel. He's not some drug-addled lap-dancer—he's a professional smartarse."

I was mildly insulted by that. I can adjust my jargon to circumstance as well as any other intellectual chameleon, and I can rabbit on about David Bohm and Roger Penrose with the best of them, if I feel the need. If the occasion were sufficiently desperate, I could even masquerade as a postmodernist for at least twenty minutes without cracking a smile. I was, however, interested to know that at last one of their previous experimental subjects had been a drug-addled lap-dancer. I might have followed that up if Claire hadn't pulled up at the hotel while she was tearing me off a strip.

"We'll get you checked in and give you ten minutes to freshen up," Lionel said. "Then we'll meet you in the lobby and take you out to the lab. Bring the CDs down with you."

Claire and Axel stayed in the car while Lionel accompanied me to the hotel desk, so I had the opportunity to say: "Where did you find those two? And why do they think that it'll help their careers to appear on *Fortean TV*?"

"They found me," he explained, as I signed the register. "They heard me on local radio and thought I might be able to put them in touch with useful subjects."

"Like me?"

"Not initially, no. You're more of a balancing factor. The lap-dancer wasn't one of mine, though. And they don't want to be on *Fortean TV*—at least, they haven't said so."

I collected my key. "It's bad enough having to sit in a chair for hours on end with cloven ping pong balls over my eyes," I told him, "without having to be insulted as well. Or are they just running a good cop/bad cop routine to soften me up? I didn't think experimental psychologists went in for intensive interrogation techniques."

"You started it," he reminded me. I took his point. My cavalier urge to show off had led me to be more than a trifle unkind to poor Axel; Claire had only been trying to restore the balance. I resolved to be more courteous in future, although I knew that it wasn't a resolution I'd find it easy to keep.

"Ten minutes," Lionel said, as I opened the door of my room.

"Not a moment longer," I promised.

* * * * * * *

I was two minutes late, not because I need any more freshening up than the next man but because I'd taken a few minutes out while contemplating the walls of my dismal hotel room to wonder why I had come all the way to Pontypridd for a lousy fifty quid. Real people don't work for fees as miserable as that, but anyone who's been a professional writer for thirty-seven years has standards some way below floor-level, and writers are also the only people in the world who can spend time productively while sitting in a comfy chair with cloven ping pong balls taped over their eyes and whatever hair they have left tidily gathered into an electrode-rich net.

Maybe, I thought, my fictitious genetic engineers could follow up their first philosophical triumphs by producing further hosts of bookworms designed to convert psychology textbooks into more traditional collections of fairy tales, self-help manuals into dictionaries and the *Fortean Times* into *Viz*.

We drove past three more abandoned pitheads and five unconvincingly-reclaimed slagheaps on the way to the university site which housed the lab where Claire and Axel committed their meager research grants to the Great Academic Drain. For some reason, the sight reminded me of my youth, when I used to sit atop Bingley Moor with my cousin Keith and look out over the Aire Valley at all the busy mills and chimneys belching black smoke into the sky. Last time I'd been back to the neighborhood Salt's Mill had enjoyed sole dominion for miles around, preserved against the march of progress by its conversion into a David Hockney museum.

The lab into which I was eventually ushered had a bad case of the Frankenstein syndrome. As Saint Oscar obligingly pointed out, life imitates art far more frequently and far more assiduously than art imitates life; ever since James Whale dressed the set of Colin Clive's monster-factory, real-world laboratories have been trying hard to emulate it. The chair didn't look too intimidating in spite of the network of electrodes draped over the head-rest and the electroencephalograph stationed behind it, and the sound-system wouldn't have looked out of place in a yuppie's loft, but the other apparatus—the one responsible for the non-invasive "further phase" that Axel had left carefully unspecified—looked seriously weird. It put me in mind of a 1920s radio set designed by Salvador Dali in the course of a particularly bad acid trip.

"What's that?" I asked.

"It's the olfactory equivalent of the synthesizer and mixer," Claire said, with brutal oversimplicity. I guessed right away that she meant the synthesizer and mixer in the sound system, which would be used to fuse my music with the hypnostream tape, but it took me a moment or two to figure out what the "olfactory equivalent" of that must be.

"You mean that it synthesizes and mixes odors," I said. "A refinement of the sort of thing supermarkets use to pipe fresh bread smells onto the sales floor."

"That's right," said Axel. "Food science has come on by leaps and bounds in the last ten years, and much of what we think of as taste is really smell. I'm not allowed to tell you which of the big food companies' R & D people loaned it to us, but it's what they call an *experiential enhancer*. The idea is...."

"I get the idea," I assured him. "Smell is the most primitive of the senses—the one that can dive down into your psyche to the deep strata of memory. It's Proust and the Madeleine, except that you want to go a lot deeper than that, into layers of fossilized race-memory, where the rich black anthracite of eternity is stored...allegedly."

"Well," said Axel, dropping the good cop act for the first time, "that's not quite...."

"Leave it, Axel," Claire said. "Let's not plant any suggestions."

"God forbid," I said. "Oh, sorry, Lionel." As an ordained minister in the Church of Wales, Lionel presumably had his own ideas about the nature and opinions of the Cosmic Mind. I wondered if he'd done his stint in the chair yet, and whether he'd caught the scent of God—or, indeed, a whiff of brimstone—but I didn't want to ask in case Claire Louchon started accusing him of planting suggestions.

"No problem," Lionel said, manifesting his invariable generosity and tolerance.

"Well," said Claire, as she studied the five CDs I'd handed over to her, "I can see that you're not intimidated by the possibility of being turned into a gibbering wreck by Lovecraftian cosmic horror."

"If I wanted to go that way," I said, I'd have brought *Andy Williams' Greatest Hits, Perry Como Sings the Blues*, and *Songs from the Best Broadway Musicals of 1959*. I don't actually have anything by Kylie or Robbie Williams." I didn't actually have the three titles I'd named, either, but that didn't seem particularly relevant to the point I was making.

Before they applied the shards of the ruined ping pong ball Axel showed me the last item of relevant equipment: a tiny tape-recorder whose mike would be clipped to the collar of my shirt. "Say anything you like," he said. "We're not expecting a running commentary on your experiences, although you can do that if you like. It's just a matter of covering the angles."

"I was wondering how you were going to obtain and analyze your results," I confessed. "I'm not sure that asking me what it was like once you've taken the blinkers off will generate anything that would pass for expert testimony, and all you're going to get from the EEG is few graphic jiggles."

"If we manage to send you where we hope to send you," Axel informed me, with a slight sigh, "the experience will probably be indescribable—at least to begin with."

"What's that supposed to mean?" I asked.

"If the run is successful, we'll invite you back, of course. This is a just a trial for the long-term project. If you measure up, we'll sign you up for monthly sessions over a year and a half. We'll bring in more sophisticated apparatus, and we'll work out a system of reportage. The pay's lousy, as you know—but it's interesting work, in its way. The subjects we've recruited so far think it'll do them some good, but we know you'd never admit that even if you were secretly persuaded of it. That's why we need you on the team, if you qualify."

"I won't," I said.

"Utterly unsuggestible," he said. "Mind like a nuclear bunker. We know. But the EEG will tell us what's really going on, no matter what extremes of denial your self-consciousness resorts to. Is it okay if I put the blinders on, now?"

I glanced sideways at Lionel, who grinned broadly and gave me a thumbs-up sign. Claire was fiddling with the EEG equipment, but the way the light was reflecting off her blue-tinted glasses would have made it difficult to know whether she was meeting my eye even if she had been that way inclined.

"Fire away," I said, relaxing into the comfy chair and closing my eyes.

"From now on," Axel said, "just forget we're here."

"No problem," I assured him, manifesting my own not-quite-invariable generosity and tolerance.

* * * * * * *

The first phase of the relaxation tape consisted of a heartbeat set against a background of quasi-oceanic white noise. The thinking behind that was easy enough to understand; it was supposed to recapitulate the preconscious but unforgotten experience of an embryo in the womb, which we are all supposed to carry within us, in the remotest depths of our memories, no matter how old we become or how comprehensively divorced from the primitive roots of our own inner being. At fifty-four, I'm a little further removed from my ancestral child than your average drug-addled lap dancer, but that only meant that I would need a little more exposure. In time, if the EEG ever testified that my brain waves had been lulled into a false sense of security, I figured that Axel and Claire would start feeding in familiar melodies to complement and complicate the fundamental rhythm without overwhelming it.

It occurred to me that blending the essential sounds of Mummy Dearest and Tinnitus of Time with the Fields of the Nephilim and the Gardens of Delight—not to mention Ataraxia and Sopor Aeternus, aided and inspired by the Ensemble of Shadows—might produce some strange results. Running through the names like that made me realize that my selections hadn't been at all inappropriate to the task in hand—probably better, I flattered myself by thinking, than anything that the terrible two's other hapless subjects had come up with.

I wasn't afraid of becoming bored, even if the relaxation tape never took effect. One of the few advantages of accepting a vocation as a writer, apart from licensing all kinds of obsessive/compulsive behavior, is that boredom becomes impossible. When you have nothing else to occupy your mind, you can get down to serious work—in fact, you can't help but get down to serious work. You don't actually have to make a mental resolution to start plotting; it happens anyway. A little bit of conscious guidance and a certain amount of extrapolative discipline help to nudge the process in more productive directions, but they aren't strictly necessary. Nor do you need to carry your "ideas" file around in your head ready for flicking through; a fertile mind may grow nothing but weeds if it's too long unattended, but they spring up in much greater profusion than they do on the average mental slag-heap. There's always something pushing up through a writer's mental subsoil, hungry for the rays of the interior sun, and if you root through it long enough, you'll always come up with something usable.

So I thought about the possibility that mice engineered as disease-models might be persuaded in future to be increasingly better mimics of human disorders, perhaps to the point of being "homunculized" by homeobox technology, and what might happen as the pressure of need required the homunculi to get larger and larger in order to better simulate the brain, and what new hazards they might be subjected to as prion-weapons were unleashed in plague war, and whether I could spin the details in such a way as to license borrowing "I am the very model of a modern Major-General" from *The Pirates of Penzance* as a title....

Then I started thinking about the possibility of writing a story about the future of biopiracy, as the big multinational pharmaceutical companies sent their privateers running riot throughout the third world in search of untapped seams of biotech treasure, harassed all the while by local buccaneers who hawked their stolen goods in some kind of futuristic Tortuga, and whether I could use *The Second Coming of Columbus* as a title, and whether, if I did, it would be worth introducing a whole new breed of ecoterrorists determined not to repeat the errors of the ill-fated Carib Indians—and who, in that case, would play Friday to whose Crusoe?—or whether it would be better to exploit the Byronic imagery of *The Corsair* or the Wagneresque brio of *The Flying Dutch-*

man, if only I could think of a crime sufficiently unusual to justify some such punishment....

It wasn't until that point, strangely enough, that I first noticed the contribution of Axel's odor-machine. Whether it was because he'd held it back until my EEG trace suggested that I was in a receptive mood or because my everpresent allergic rhinitis had preventing me from smelling the introductory suite of odors I had no idea. The first odor I recognized, however, was wood smoke. It would be claiming too much to say that I recognized any others, but I did get a suggestion of dry and slightly acrid grass, with a slight seasoning of musk and shit. It didn't take a genius to work out that Axel was trying to recapitulate the perfume of the African savannah where our remote ancestors had first evolved as primal biotechnologists, developing all the tools and skills required for cooking and making clothes.

Then the odors faded again, or became too weird to classify. Either way, I lost interest and went back to work.

I began thinking about human chimeras, compounded as early embryos out of egg-cells donated by as many as eight or twelve genetically-enhanced parents, which would allow the aggregate households of the emortality-challenged future to conserve a biological relationship between parents and children, and what might then happen if the various cell-stocks began a kind of battle to constitute the different tissues and organs of the chimerical individual, and how the eight or twelve parents might feel as they monitored the results of that conflict and witnessed the settlements of a kind of natural selection that had never had a chance to occur before, and whether the conflict might reach resolutions previously unimagined if the chimerical wholes began manufacturing transposons in order to facilitate their own internal gene-trading mechanisms....

Then I wasted a little time on trivia, wondering whether cultures currently practicing clitoridectomy might take advantage of a rapid increase of expertise in embryonic engineering by requesting that their female children should be modified in the womb in such a way that that they wouldn't require any such surgical operation, and what effects that might have on the consequent generation of declitorized female infants...and whether, if ambitious chimerization became possible at the same time as sophisticated embryonic engineering, lycanthropy might one day become fashionable, at least until the werewolves' innate gene-trading systems began to exercise a distinct preference for wolfishness...in much the same way that the embryonically-modified clitoris-free children might decide to take charge of their own future development and evolution by continuing the process which their blinkered parents had only begun, without even bothering to wonder what further consequences there might be once the snowball started rolling....

I got a whiff of something slightly noxious at this point, which put me in mind of a Lovecraftian shoggoth, but somewhere in the distance Francesca Nicoli of Ataraxia was singing the dolphin song from *Lost Atlantis*, so I knew that everything was fundamentally right with the world and that I wasn't yet in danger of hearing the call of Cthulhu. After a moment or two it faded, and I got back to work yet again.

I began wondering whether I might be able to make a story out of the dramatically-increased mutation-rates suffered by so-called mammoth genes with ten or more introns, and whether the importation of new mammoth genes to plants or animals might be used as a mechanism to speed up evolution, especially in association with artificial transposons, and whether the double meaning of mammoth might help supply a plot as well as a title, especially if I could make out a case for prehistoric mammoths having fallen into an evolutionary trap because their own lack of mammoth genes condemned them to an inflexibility from which a dose thereof might have saved them, and what might have become of the populations of pre-Ice Age Europe if some such dose of mutagenic potential had been provided by a comet from the Oort Cloud exploding in the atmosphere somewhere over Denmark, allowing Neanderthalers to become supermen who not only domesticated mammoths and saber-toothed tigers but became masters of mutational husbandry, pharmacogenetic alchemy and *authentic* transcendental trancing and dancing as the ice retreated and the world became Sumerland again....

And so on.

The Haunted Bookshop, by Brian Stableford

* * * * * * *

Eventually, Axel Castle removed the two halves of the bisected ping pong ball from my face and said, with a heartfelt sigh: "Well, it's early days yet."

I heard the echoes of Carl McCoy's distorted voice fading away from the contrapuntal melody to leave the synthetic heartbeat in full possession of my earphones.

"I did relax," I told him. "I got as close to trance as I ever do, dancing as merrily as I can without actually tapping my feet."

"It's okay," he said. "The first run is always a bust. It takes people a couple of hours to get used to the equipment. Tomorrow, we'll be in with a chance. Tonight, we might as well go for a pizza."

He was as good as his word. We all went for a pizza.

Until you've had an authentic Welsh pizza, cooked in an oven lined with authentic Pontypridd slate, topped with all the most gorgeous produce of the valleys, including nutty slack and lamb's testicles, washed down with water from the sacred Snowdonian spring which nourished the voice of Taliesin and the Bardic custodians of Druidic tradition, you haven't lived....

Well, actually, I made that last bit up—all the sober reportage was getting me down, so I thought I'd relax by throwing in an improbability or two. I'll be sure to let you know if and when we get to the other one, because I have my reputation to think of—after all, what kind of writer would use himself as an unreliable narrator?

The rumor that you can order laverbread as a topping in Welsh pizza parlors is grossly exaggerated; actually, you can't—except, maybe, in Haverfordwest. What you can get in certain parts of Wales, though, on certain nights of the year, if you're really lucky, is Lionel Fanthorpe's after-dinner conversation, which is never less than hugely entertaining, even if he does mention God occasionally.

We ran through the usual gamut of anecdotes about everyone scheduled to appear on the next series of *Fortean TV*, the plots of all 186 of Lionel's Badger books—except for the one he couldn't remember, which he probably hadn't actually written—and the recent exploits of his family, friends, acquaintances, and pets. Then he sang a few songs, punctuated by profuse apologies for having left his guitar in Cardiff.

It was great fun, especially watching Claire and Axel trying to get the occasional word in edgewise after Lionel had built up a (purely metaphorical) full head of steam. Had the opportunity arisen to inform them that their only hope was to rotate the word in question into the fourth dimension and then slip it back through a chronoclastic double pleat while he was drawing breath I would have, but it never did.

On the way back to the hotel, though, I found myself in the back of the Hyundai with Axel.

"Did I say anything into the tape recorder?" I asked. I figured that the tape might be useful if I'd managed to jot down a few useful plot ideas.

"Not a word," he assured me. "You relaxed, but the walls separating your little ego-fragment from the Cosmic Mind didn't even crack, let alone crumble. You're used to the set-up now, though. 'Tomorrow is another day', as Scarlett O'Hara said to Rhett Butler."

"No she didn't," I told him. "Rhett was long gone by then. She said it to the little girl—or maybe the land. Well, actually, she said it to the reader...it's a writer's mission to educate his readers—or her readers, in Margaret Mitchell's case—in the utility of idiotic platitudes. It's a dark and lonely job, but somebody has to do it. Or is that mining?"

"Not around these parts," Axel said dryly. "Not any more. Nine o'clock in the morning too early for you?"

"No problem," I assured him, as the Hyundai pulled up outside my hotel.

* * * * * * *

The breakfast was as classy as the hotel, which is the only good thing you can say about British hotels in general. All I can ever be bothered to get for myself at home is a bowl of cereal, so it made a nice change to fill up on overstuffed sausages, crispy bacon, congealed fried eggs, slushy tomatoes, and greasy fried bread. I was careful not to overdose on the coffee, though; I didn't want to get restless legs while I was sitting in the comfy chair in my hi-tech hairnet staring into the cloudy interior of the divided ping pong ball.

I wondered briefly whether the ping pong ball that had been so cruelly sacrificed upon the Altar of Science was sufficiently in tune with the relentless surge of the Cosmic Mind to yearn for its lost wholeness, but figured that it probably wasn't. If I were a ping pong ball, I decided, I'd probably be grateful to take on the kind of work that one was now doing, even if it meant being split in two; it had to be better than being ceaselessly bashed back and forth across a table, bouncing first on this side and then on that—except when being served, in which case there would be an extra bounce accompanied by a particularly dizzying spin. What sort of existence would that be? It would, I decided, be almost as bad as being the element in an electric kettle.

"Where's Lionel?" I asked, when Claire's Hyundai rolled up and Axel invited me to get into the front seat.

"He had to do his early-morning spot on the radio, and half a dozen other things. It's Saturday, after all. He told us to look after you and to tell you that he'd try to pop into the railway station to say goodbye, but that he couldn't promise."

"Fair enough," I said. "Let's go see the Cosmic Mind. Or do I mean the Wizard of Oz? It's difficult to tell whether the road's made of yellow brick when there's so much grime around."

"Pontypridd is a clean town by comparison with some," Claire said, severely.

"I know," I said, although a lot of shit had flown into the sewer since I'd last seen Bolton-on-Dearne. "I am going to give this a go, you know. I'll relax as far as I possibly can. I just can't offer any guarantees. I really don't take suggestions very easily."

"That's why we asked you," she reminded me.

This time, I sneaked a closer look at the odor-manufacturing equipment. One console with knobs on looks pretty much like another, and the mess of glass and plastic tubing leading to a mutant filter-funnel—which, I presumed, was where the carefully-engineered fumes came out to play in the otherwise=sterile atmosphere—looked like nothing I'd ever seen or dreamed of before, so I wasn't in any position to make productive comparisons, let alone to estimate its power or its subtlety. The synthesizer and mixer hooked up in the sound-system seemed distinctly user-friendly by comparison. I wondered whether I might have done better to bring *Bringing It All Back Home*, so that I could go dancing with *Mr. Tambourine Man* and investigate the *Gates of Eden*, but figured that another trip to Lost Atlantis would probably do almost as well, and that if "Last Exit for the Lost" couldn't take me out of myself nothing was ever likely to.

"Okay?" Axel said, as he covered my eyes.

"Peachy," I assured him. "As a matter of interest, did the drug-addled lap-dancer make the team for the six-month tour?"

"Oh yes," he said. "Might have been born for trancing. A real natural. If anyone can get to and beyond bliss, it's her. We have high hopes."

"Doesn't fill one with confidence about the Cosmic Mind's IQ, does it?" I sniped. "Doesn't exactly make one keen to snuggle up in the universal bosom, either. Imagine how disappointing it would be to get back in touch with the Ultimate only to find that the entire universe has a bad case of Alzheimer's Entropy complicated by Spiritual Syphilis."

"Imagine how much it will appreciate your input, then," Axel murmured. "Ready for the big beat?"

I was.

* * * * * * *

As Axel had shrewdly pointed out, I was used to the apparatus now. It was familiar. It's amazing how quickly repetition can turn into ritual, how casually one can discard a reflexive sense of unease. It was only the second time I'd sat in the comfy chair, but it felt perfectly familiar, and as soon as the fake heartbeat got into its measured stride I had the sensation of recovering something whose absence, though unnoticed, had been troubling me at some subconscious level.

Let's see, I thought. *Where was I, exactly...?*

THE HAUNTED BOOKSHOP, BY BRIAN STABLEFORD

For at least ten thousand years, I reminded myself, mental and social evolution had outstripped the physiological evolution of a body whose emotional equipment was shaped by brutality. In the future of genetic engineering, however, physiological evolution would far outstrip the mental and social evolution of a brain whose moral equipment had been shaped by terror. That was the world for which the modern mind ought to be preparing itself, and it needed all the help it could get, even from science fiction...and that was why I wasn't wasting my time while I sat in the midst of this mock-Frankensteinian set-up. I might not be going beyond bliss— or, for that matter, getting within a million miles of bliss— but there was a sense in which I was more closely in touch with the heartbeat and muscle of the Cosmos than any hallucinogen-soaked and endorphin-drenched trace-and-dancer was ever likely to be...or so, at least, I had to believe if I were to continue to take myself seriously, or even if I were to continue to think of my babbling-brook-of-consciousness as a tale worth retailing, a narrative worth reviewing, a seam worth seeming. Whether there was, in fact, a Cosmic Mind or not—and whether, if so, one could meet it without dissolving into a puddle of Lovecraftian *angst*—there was work to be done in picking away at the coal-face of the futuristic imagination, hewing fuel for the fires of the intellect that would burn far brighter, in spite of its blackness, than any heap of twigs amassed by a curious ape on the African plain...or, for that matter, any pitiless Jurassic sun, whose reptile-favoring glare never dreamed of eclipse...or even any submarine volcanic flux stirring the primal mud into the first repetitive semblances of life....

However comfortable I had become in the seductive arms of Axel Castle's mind-blowing kit, I needed to work... to plan...to plot....

Oddly enough, though, the kinds of plot that came drifting into my mind as I did my level best to play the game, and relax to the point at which Axel and Claire might think that they'd got their fifty quid's worth out of me, weren't the same kinds of plots that had drifted into my mind the previous day. Those had been science fiction plots, extrapolating rationally plausible ideas with at least a modicum of scrupulous sensitivity. The ideas that now rose up from the unconscious for aesthetic appraisal were ideas of another and more intellectually anarchic kind.

I thought about Biggles, in his earliest incarnation as a pilot in World War I, taking his Sopwith Camel into a weird cloud while being chased by Spads on night patrol, and being temporarily displaced into a marginal dimension, where the exhaust fumes of his engine begin to take on demonic form, as if attempting to gain some kind of substance, to become *dust*, as the first step on an evolutionary ladder that would lead to an invasion of the human realm by predatory monsters....

The advantage of stories like that, of course, is that they have their endings already built-in. On the previous day, I'd had difficulty carrying any of my ideas through to anything that looked like a respectable narrative closure; the trouble with futuristic fiction is that the future never ends, being fully occupied in eternal processes of beginning and becoming. Fantasy, light or dark, is very different; fantasy is always end-orientated, always the produce of wishes and fears, always aimed at fulfillment or escape, and the writer's job is merely to organize a pleasing trajectory or an ingenious obstacle course to delay the inevitable consummation.

All that Biggles has to do, therefore, is fly out of the cloud again, to return to the bright and bitter normality of the Spad-filled skies. A nightmare, however nasty, has only to be dispelled, even if its motifs always leave a hint behind to remind the characters and the reader that the threat of dissolution is still there and always will be. Nowadays, you aren't allowed to accomplish that fictive sleight-of-hand that by having your protagonist wake up to the discovery that he's been asleep, but there are any number of ways of achieving the transition deceptively...and it's always there, drawing the tale like a lodestone the size of the Earth.

I could smell something, but it wasn't the savannah. I couldn't make it out, but I didn't know whether its enigmatic quality was subjective or objective. Non-invasive, Axel had said, and completely harmless, so it couldn't be ether or chloroform or anything that was going to send me to the Land of Dreams, even in combination with a saraband for dead lovers or an excursion to Bosch's Garden of Delight—which is, after all, the world as it is, colored by the human imagination, safely set aside from heaven and hell. It was probably the effect of my allergy, I thought, that was preventing me recognizing the odor, although I doubted that it would evoke a memory even if I had the nose of a hungry hyena.

I thought about a musician, perhaps a composer, perhaps half of some Gothesque duo, who acquires an elusive stalker, perhaps glimpsing some female figure in black who always disappears in the shadows, but who also manifests herself in enigmatic e-mails and cryptic answerphone messages, who might be some kind of vampiric muse or some kind of melomaniac creature instinctively attracted by his work, and with whom he becomes obsessed in either case, unable to shake the idea that he might gift her the extra substance she lacks and so fervently desires, if only at cost of his own....

That story too, and all its routine variants, had its ending built in. The musician/composer/painter/writer has to die, of course, after the long fade to grey, exhausting himself in his futile quest and thus abstracting himself from a world in which he doesn't really belong, from which he himself is dispelled in spite of having to do it by being spelled, correctly or not, in a world where enchantment is given a poetic license to work...that being, of course, the very nature of fantasy....

Then I thought about a nineteenth century whore who learns to see the fairy folk as her syphilis develops into its tertiary, mind-rotting phase, and realizes by degrees that she is now the Queen of Elfland...except that Faerie Queens only reign for a single day before being sacrificed and their blood scattered on the fields where forbidden fruit are grown...although that isn't as inconvenient as it sounds, because a day in Faerie is seven years on Earth and lasts every bit as long, subjectively speaking, provided that you can hear the music playing, which is easy enough if you can only force the fiddlers to keep on playing and the rhymers to keep on singing and the dancers to keep on and on and on....

And stories like that have perfectly natural endings, because they have a fixed span built into them from the very

THE HAUNTED BOOKSHOP, BY BRIAN STABLEFORD

beginning, which only has to run its allotted course like fate or destiny or a chapter-by-chapter plan roughed out on the back of an old envelope. The whore has to die, of course, because that's what syphilis does to whores, but that's not the point of this kind of story, which is that the brute facts of vicious reality needn't figure if you have a way to get around them by slipping into the nth dimension and flying edgewise as far away from the world as wings of desire will take you, even if you know that sooner or later you'll flutter into a chronofantastic whirlpool and come bouncing back into the world, spinning like mad, to resume the game of serve-smash-and-bounce, serve-smash-and-bounce....

I thought I could see something inside the blinkers, but I knew that it was only something within my eyes, like hypnagogic or hypnopompic imagery, or phosphenes, or...was that tune really one of mine, or had Claire slipped in something of her own? And what was that musty smell, damp and dark? Air captured in a deep coal-mine? Something scraped from the inner brickwork of a dynamited chimney? Fungus dredged from the depths of glutinous soil? Bacteria dredged from the marine abyss, from the lip of a black smoker?

So I thought about making a deal with a demon, under inconvenient circumstances because Satan is dead as a result of a second war in Heaven and the demon no longer has any real interest in human souls, although he might be willing to trade a few magical favors for a share of the summoner's bodily experience, to which the narrator will naturally agree because that's the kind of guy he is, with the result that while in possession of him, the demon confers a visionary talent on his summoner, which has a permanent effect far outlasting the culmination of the deal, and which renders the aforementioned magical favors redundant by overwriting all the appetites that they might have served....

Which is what qualifies as an ironic twist in stories of that sort, which always end in ironic twists because that's the kind of story they are, there not being much call for demons in horror stories any more, since TV overkill reduced them all to the status of infusoria-ex-machina, although all horror eventually turns into comedy anyhow, because that's what a sense of humor is for, if you really think about it...which you really ought to, even if it doesn't look like a useful source of new plots, because there has to be more to life than work after all, if there's any sense in which a writer can ever stop working, which there probably isn't....

Or maybe the demon story could avoid the bathetic twist, and put on a cloak of metaphysical pretension, presuming that there's something profound in the idea of a reconfigured cosmos in which Heaven and Hell are obsolete and a whole new metaphysical "superstructure" is in the making, reflecting the changing pattern of human understanding, anxiety and yearning, in which everything would be reconfigured, including and especially the Cosmic Mind, which wouldn't be subdivided on any crude Freudian lines into a deistic superego and a diabolical id, or any mere set of quasi-Jungian archetypes, but would be something more along the lines of the mind of sentient Cosmos conceivable in a scientific world-view that can dream such things as the implicate order and the quantum theory of the will and the Omega Point and the inflationary universe and all the lovely jargon of quarks and beauty, strangeness and charm....

Which is, when you think about it, I told myself, what all this really ought to be about. Eternity's Eve...yet another chance to deploy a title you've been trying to fit a story to for years. A universe infinitely replicating itself as the Cosmic Mind searches for an original idea, a story that doesn't have its ending ready built-in, while memory leakage reacquaints the favored children of eternity with their former lives and former mistakes and makes them dream of trance and dance and transcendence and all its echoes in out-of-body experiences, flight and cosmic voyages through space and time and worlds in which the dead are afraid of coming to life again and losing the refined, sensitive emotional spectrum of the dead to infection by love and greed, pain and joy, and all the other afflictions of the tumorous flesh that grows like mould upon their bones while existential angst caused by the terror of life runs riot in their utterly sane and rational minds, and plagues of bookworms devour the ink of diaries and registers of birth and death, newspapers and financial accounts, junk mail and parliamentary reports, excreting it all as an infinite epic poem whose lines surge and swell to

The Haunted Bookshop, by Brian Stableford

the rhythm of the spheres, telling tales of all the heroes there ever were, and all the accomplishments they ever made on behalf of all the folks back home, that being what heroes are and what heroes do, whose stories never ever end....

The Cosmic Mind, when you really think about it, I thought, is more ancient than the stars whose dust we are, and yet is young...so very young, so very ambitious, so magnificently and triumphantly dead that it need never fear any return to meager life, nor any conclusive extinction while it has the power to form a single thought...that thought being, according to tradition, *fiat lux*, except that the author of that particular scriptural passage probably misheard what was being dictated to him, which was in fact *fiat luxe*, the Cosmic Mind knowing all languages and not being afraid of any miscegenation, any more than it could ever be content with mere light when it could have luxury instead...and what is a universe, after all, but luxury incarnate, especially a universe minded to contain life as well as light, so fertile with its power of invention as to image the ascent of cyanobacterial slime on a tide of *élan vital* to be the kind of being who is sufficiently fond of himself—or herself—to imagine that getting back in touch with the Cosmic Mind might be an experience as rewarding as an acid trip or a lap dance or a combination of the two, when anyone with half a brain or half a ping pong ball can smell and see the obvious conclusion that we ought not to be content with tales with obvious conclusions, which lead inexorably to fulfillments or escapes, when what we ought to be concerned with is an infinitude of beginnings and becomings and making ourselves more human than we already are, more divided than we already are, more separate and secluded and busy and immune to boredom than we already are, because anyone who actually did go beyond bliss to bathe in the all-encompassing climax of the Cosmic Mind would have reached a conclusion to which there was no conceivable sequel, a punctuation mark which permitted no continuation, a completeness whose aesthetic neatness would be tantamount to annihilation, beyond comedy or tragedy, *lux* or *luxe* or lucks or looks...beyond even wordplay—which is to say, a return to the Void.

THE HAUNTED BOOKSHOP, BY BRIAN STABLEFORD

I could smell blood—which was not, as it turned out, a good thing, at least from the point of view of the experimenters who were paying me, though not very well, for my valuable time.

* * * * * * *

"Okay," said Axel, with one of his oh-so-patient sighs. "We give up."

Light flooded my eyes. Somewhere in the distance I could hear Artaud Franzmann wailing about *Necromanteion*, so faintly that the words could hardly penetrate the thunderous pulse of the world whose melody they were trying so plaintively to provide.

Then that was gone too. And the hair-net.

"You were right," Axel said. "You're never going to get there. Your brain just can't let go. Bliss is not for you. As for what might lie beyond bliss...well, we'll just have to leave that to the lap-dancers, won't we?"

"They're not all lap dancers, are they?" I said.

"Every last one of them," he said, before adding: "Just kidding."

I picked up a scalpel from the bench and split his skull in two like a fractured ping pong ball, with a single dexterous sweep of my right hand. There was blood everywhere, and the blood was green. As Axel's mask of flesh dissolved, I saw the alien creature within the human shell: the unspeakable compound of all things loathsome. It could have been a shoggoth, but how was I to know? Claire screamed, then dropped dead, the life having been frightened right out of her. Psychologists are so impressionable.

Well, actually, I made that bit up. I did warn you that I might. In reality, I'm not the violent type. This time, though, I wasn't straining under the awful yoke of sober reportage and longing to be free; I just thought you might like a dramatic climax, and a clear-cut ending. Some readers do. If you're one of them, you might as well stop now, and forget that you read this paragraph. Hold on to the idea of the shoggoth, and everything going to hell, or to the image of the hero bravely gripping his *deus ex machina*, having saved the world from the invention that food science was not meant to know...whichever suits you best. The rest of the actual story is, I fear, far too plausible for its own good.

"So I didn't make the team," I said to the world-weary experimentalist. "No recall for the writer."

"Don't be too disappointed," Axel said. "We'll find a skeptic somewhere whose brain isn't quite as set in its ways as yours. Lionel gave us a few more names. I'll write you a check, but you'll have to give me a receipt."

It wasn't quite as dispiriting as the time I got invited to dinner with the government's chief scientific adviser and had to turn him down because I was teaching in Winchester on the evening in question, but it was close. It shouldn't have been; after all, not having to take part in the long-term program would save me a lot of time and a certain amount of hassle, and might even guarantee that I would never see Pontypridd again as long as I lived.

But even so....

"Given another hour or so," I told the terrible two, while they drove me back to the station, "I think I might have come up with a few usable plot ideas. Which reminds me—did you get anything on the tape this time?"

"Only humming," Claire told me. "I think you were murmuring along to your CDs. You must have been bored."

"I don't get bored," I told her, severely. "I'm a writer." I looked out of the side window to emphasize my ability to transcend unpromising circumstance.

Somehow, the abandoned pitheads seemed more poignant now than they had before, and the thought of those lonely seams of unappreciated anthracite, buried deeper than bliss, was almost too much to bear.

"Maybe that's the problem, Dr. Stableford," Axel chirped up from the back of the Hyundai. "Your mind just stays busy, even when it's locked away on its own."

He repeated all this to Lionel when we got to the platform from which the eastbound train was scheduled to depart in ten minutes. Lionel had been waiting for us there for some little while, eager for a chance to say goodbye. He was politely interested in Axel's diagnosis of my problem, and eager to help if he could. "You might try a little yoga," he suggested. You need to get reconnected. Perhaps it's not your skepticism that's holding you back—perhaps it's more that you keep on thinking, long after a sensible person would have stopped for a rest, even when there's nowhere for the train of thought to go but on and on and on. Still, it was good of you to come, and it's always good to see you."

"You too," I told him. "I'm glad you asked me. The trip wasn't a total loss, no matter what your friends might think. A change is as good as a rest. Give me a ring next time you need a skeptical observer. If I'm free...."

Claire Louchon had to have the last word, of course. She looked at me through her blue-tinted spectacles as my train came in and said: "The trouble with you, Dr. Stableford, is that you're too self-contained. That's why you'll never get in touch with the Cosmic Mind. That's why you'll never get as far as bliss, let alone beyond it."

"Oh dear," I said. "Silly me. What a pity. Still...never mind."

THE HAUNTED BOOKSHOP, BY BRIAN STABLEFORD

ALL YOU INHERIT

The first time Amelia saw her dead mother was on the stroke of midnight on the June night when she lost her virginity in the back seat of Jason Stringer's dad's Mondeo and fell pregnant with Lisa. It was very dark in the car—which was parked inside Jason Stringer's dad's garage—but not so dark that Amelia couldn't see her mother peering around the plastic headrest on top of the front passenger seat.

Her mother looked as if she were thirty again, with hardly a line in her face and her hair full, soft and luxurious. She was shaking her luxuriously-dressed head sorrowfully.

"You silly girl," she said. "You silly, *silly* Millie."

Amelia was slightly hurt. Given that she was over the age of consent—if only by a little bit—and had always exhibited exceptional precocity in non-sex-related matters, she felt that she was fully entitled to be criticized in a more mature manner. What her mother *should* have said was, "You stupid cow. You bloody stupid *cow*"—but being Amelia's mum she just had to say what she said in terms which implied that Amelia was still a cocksure little girl putting up a front of cleverness, which she wasn't. Hadn't she just proved it?

"I'll be all right, Mum," Amelia assured her mother, and honestly thought that perhaps it would, even though she knew perfectly well that what she'd just done was risky.

"That's what *I* thought," her mother replied, as if that were nailed-down proof that Amelia had got it wrong. "I was just as clever as you. I could have been a *contender*."

Amelia knew that she should have made sure that she was protected, but she just hadn't known exactly how to go about it. She had grasped the fundamental concept of contraception, of course, but she didn't know how you actually got up the nerve to do it in a calculated manner, either by asking the doctor or asking the boy. If her mother had been alive, maybe she could have asked her, but somehow she doubted it. It wouldn't have been any easier to ask Mum than to go to the doctor or demanded that Jason go to the chemist's. Any of those strategies of preparation would have required far more courage than it took simply to open her legs and let Jason bring to a head, so to speak, all of the pressure that had been bearing down on her for months.

She didn't even fancy Jason, particularly, and she didn't imagine that he had any particular affection for her. He and she were both old enough to know that only twenty per cent of boys and twenty per cent of girls were really and truly fanciable, and that people who weren't in the relevant twenty per cents just had to make do. She had to do it some day, and so did he, just to get it out of the way and get on with life, and it had just been a matter of blundering around until an occasion presented itself at a time when one person's determination was running high and another person's resistance was running low and both of them happened to think "What the hell, go for it" at almost the same moment. Of course it was a risk, but every decision you took in life—not just the major ones but every petty day-by-day and hour-by-hour hesitation—was a risk. That was the human condition: risk piled on risk piled on risk. What good did it do to say "That's what *I* thought" as if one item of experience were enough to change the nature of life itself?

Anyway, Amelia thought, how many girls got pregnant the first time, fumbling around in the back of a car to no effect at all except to wonder what all the fuss was about and to conjure up the censorious phantom of your dead mother? Not many.

Unfortunately, Amelia Curtinshaw was one of the few.

* * * * * * *

Amelia's mother—whose name was Faith, although she was not religious—had been a victim of medical negligence three times over. That was one more reason, if any more were needed, why Amelia didn't find it easy to go to the doctor.

There was no way of knowing whether or not Faith Curtinshaw would have survived any longer if she had not been the victim of medical negligence, but Amelia's father—whose name was Merlyn, although he was not Welsh—took the view that you had to accept that doctors working under pressure occasionally made mistakes, and that it was socially irresponsible to threaten them with the law every time they lost a patient, and that the chain of misfortunes that had happened to his wife was a million-to-one-shot. The insurance company who had to pay out on Faith's premature demise suggested very strongly to Merlyn that he ought to sue the local health authority for damages, but they had no power to compel him to do it and no right to withhold payment on the policy if he chose not to, so he chose not to.

"I have to think of Amelia," he said to anyone who questioned his decision. "What would it do to her to drag the death of her mother through the courts, prolonging her agony for years and years, in the hope of winning a little blood money? Isn't it better to get on with our lives? It'd be a lottery anyway, wouldn't it? Who really wins that kind of lottery? Only the lawyers. Not the people on either side of the courtroom, and certainly not the art and science of medicine."

Merlyn Curtinshaw had a high opinion of the art and science of medicine. That was what the more ambitious boys in his class at his independent grammar school had gone on to study at university. Because he lacked their confidence, he'd settled for studying Biology and becoming a teacher, but he'd laid the foundations of a good career in an all-boys' grammar school similar in all essential respects to the one in which he'd been educated himself. In such a context, Faith once told Amelia in a moment of uncommon confidentiality, he had good reason to thank the whim of fate which had made his parents choose to spell his name with an l instead of a v. In all-boys' schools any teacher named Mervyn, even one who showed not the slightest trace of homosexual inclination, would inevitably be dubbed "Merv the Perv", whereas a teacher named Merlyn was a stone cold certainty to be nicknamed "the wizard"—as, in fact, he was.

Faith Curtinshaw had first fallen victim to medical negligence when a routine smear test had been cleared as a-okay by a laboratory in Barnsley whose staff subsequently turned out to have been overstressed, overstretched and not overly observant. When it transpired, after an interval of eighteen months, that several patients who had been given the all-clear had, in fact, been very far from a-okay, Faith was recalled, along with several thousand other women, to take another test. Because Faith's family, on Amelia's Grandma Booth's side, had something of a history of cervical cancer, she doubtless felt slightly more anxious than the thousands of other recall cases, but as she dutifully pointed out to Merlyn and Amelia, there was unlikely to be one among them who was not anxious at all.

Unfortunately, the burden imposed on a laboratory in Lichfield by the thousands of extra slides resulted in its staff becoming just as overstressed and overstretched as the staff at Barnsley. Mindful of their duty, they labored long and hard to make sure that every slide had been double-checked and every slide that excited even the slightest hint of suspicion triple-checked, but this assiduousness threw their record-keeping system into such disarray that they lost the notes of several hundred cases, including Faith's. There was nothing for it but for her to report for yet another test, whose resultant slides were eventually adjudged by a laboratory in Darlington to be very suspicious indeed, probably indicative of a serious problem.

The result of the smear-test had, of course, to be confirmed by a biopsy. Unfortunately, a laboratory in Hull contrived to lose the results of the biopsy, not because its technicians were working under enormous stress—although they were—but because of a problem with its antique computer-system, which had never recovered from the effects of a diagnostic test intended to figure out how vulnerable it would be to the Millennium bug. Faith attempted to remain calm after turning up for a second biopsy, singing "Take Another Little Piece of My Womb, why don't you?" to the tune of Janis Joplin's "Take Another Little Piece of My Heart" all the way home in Merlyn Curtinshaw's second-hand Citroen, but by that time she was absolutely convinced that the roll of the dice was against her, and that metastasis was already making hay throughout her nether regions.

"Am I going to get it?" Amelia asked, when her mother was finally diagnosed as the victim of an exceptionally aggressive cancer and went back to the hospital to start a course of chemotherapy that had no better than a one-in-three chance of being effective.

"All you inherit is the risk," Faith told her daughter. "One day, maybe fairly soon, they'll be able to test your genes to see whether you've got the duff one. If you have, you'll just have to trust to luck to avoid the little accidents that might disable its healthy partner in one of the relevant cells. If you want all the jargon, ask your father—he's the biologist."

Given the way that luck had treated her mother, Amelia didn't think that it seemed very trustworthy. Getting pregnant in the back of Jason Stringer's dad's Mondeo while it was unromantically parked in Jason Stringer's dad's garage didn't increase her faith in luck one little bit, nor even her faith in Faith's judgment.

* * * * * * *

Merlyn Curtinshaw reacted to the news of Amelia's pregnancy with predictable stoicism. He didn't call her a bloody stupid cow, or even a silly, silly girl, although he did observe that it would play havoc with her A levels. Given that she was now scheduled to give birth a full fourteen months before she was scheduled to sit her A levels, Amelia had to concede that this was true.

"What do you want to do?" he asked, meaning did she want to have an abortion, or what?

"Jason asked me to marry him when I told him," she replied, "but I said no. He's only seventeen. I suppose he's bright enough—two short planks wouldn't stand a chance against him in an IQ race—but he's not what you'd call *together*, and his parents are monsters. He might make a father in ten years time, but if we married now we'd probably be divorced in three. Did Granddad Curtinshaw ever have a Mondeo, by any chance?"

"No," said Merlyn. "He was a Vauxhall man through and through, although he wasn't from South London. Why do you ask?"

"Just something mum said. She was sitting in the front passenger seat of a Mondeo at the time." Amelia reflected that her father had probably been well and truly *together* even at seventeen, and was so together by now that he was practically set in stone.

"I can assure you that your mother would never be seen dead in the front seat of a Mondeo," her father assured her, showing how much he had still had to learn about his wife when the opportunity was rudely snatched away from him, "and you still haven't answered my question."

"I don't want an abortion," Amelia told him. "Not because I'm squeamish, or because I think it would be murder, and not because I have some bloody stupid idea about how cool it would be to be a teenage mother. I just don't want to take the risk of flushing something down the toilet that might turn out to be a-okay, if I don't actually have to. How do *you* feel?"

"I feel that you ought to be allowed to make your own decisions," he said, because he obviously knew that it was the sort of thing a good father would say. "You can count on me to do what I can. But there's one more thing I ought to tell you."

"What?"

"The reason you don't have any brothers or sisters is that your mother was afraid that having more children might increase her risk of carrying forward the family curse. That's what she called it: *carrying forward the family curse.*"

"Called what?"

"The fact that so many of her female relatives on her mother's side had died of cervical cancer. She felt—and after inspecting the data she'd gathered I had to concede the correlation—that the ones who had more children tended to die earlier. Stress to the relevant tissues, you see. Plausible argument, although I wouldn't call it scientific proof."

"But she had me," Amelia pointed out.

THE HAUNTED BOOKSHOP, BY BRIAN STABLEFORD

"Yes," said Merlyn Curtinshaw, with a tear in the corner of his left eye. "She had you. At nineteen."

Amelia noticed that he did not add, although he certainly could have, that at nineteen Faith had not yet done the genealogical research that had stoked the fire of her anxieties and made her conscious of the risks involved in merely being alive. Nor did he mention that having a child at nineteen had forced Faith Booth to drop out of university and get married, incidentally making sure that she never would be a contender in any kind of fight for fame and fortune.

That must have been a pity, Amelia thought, because Faith had probably been even brighter than her husband, who would himself have been able to give two short planks a ninety-nine yard start in a hundred-yard IQ race without having to hurry unduly.

* * * * * * *

Amelia's pregnancy was routine—and so was life at home, which had become so very routine as to be positively formal. Even while his wife was alive, Merlyn Curtinshaw had never been a particularly demonstrative father, but after Faith's death he became very wary indeed of hugging and kissing his daughter. Perhaps he would have been wary in any case, simply because she was—to borrow a phrase from the late lamented Grandma Booth—"filling out", but Amelia was bright enough to see that there were other factors involved. For one thing, a widower living with a teenage daughter had to be exceedingly careful to remain above suspicion. For another, something of Merlyn Curtinshaw that had withered when his wife died never had regained its turgor under time's supposedly healing influence.

Amelia observed that after her mother died, her father stopped complaining about the awful burden of expectation that modern society placed upon its secondary school teachers. He stopped groaning under the weight of the marking and other miscellaneous paperwork that he was forced to bring home. Indeed, his marking procedures grew increasingly conscientious. He was capable of sitting in front of the TV for hours on end, barely glancing at *EastEnders* or

Brookside (although he always seemed *au fait* with the major plot-threads) plowing through second- and third-year General Science.

"Hell, dad, it's *science*," Amelia occasionally said to him. "Either the silly little buggers have got the answers right or they haven't. What's with all the deep thought?"

"It's not as easy as that, Millie," he always replied. "I have to determine the extent to which they've understood the fundamental concepts, and to what extent erroneous answers are merely the result of sloppy calculation."

Amelia knew, however, that her father had taken to hiding within his work, immersing himself in its toils so that he did not have to engage himself with any sort of life outside the home, or to engage himself fully with life within it. He even began to take a perverse pride in his cooking, abandoning Marks & Spencer Ready Meals forever.

Every Saturday Amelia would pore over the *Guardian* "Soulmates" column on her father's behalf, diligently pointing out likely prospects, but he always treated it as a joke. Amelia had always suspected that her father wasn't very highly sexed, but she knew perfectly well that, despite her lack of siblings, his marriage to her mother had been reasonably active, even moderately joyful. It seemed to her, once her mother had been dead for more than a year, that the metastasizing claws of the crab which had eaten her mother must have been unnaturally long, and that it was not merely her mother's nether regions that had been devastated by them. It seemed to Amelia, after the incident in Jason Stringer's dad's Mondeo, that her mother probably got out of her tomb more often than her father got out of his.

Not that her father was lonely, of course, in any non-sexual sense. He had her to keep him company most nights. She got out regularly, though, until the pregnancy reached its sixth month, at which point being out got to be a bit embarrassing. She resolved then that as soon as it became practicable after Lisa was born—she had named the child as soon as a sonic scan revealed its sex—she would get out again, at least once a week. When Mrs. Lipton, the cleaning lady, quit during Amelia's eighth month, on the grounds that she hadn't time to clear up after babies and that an extra pound a week wouldn't come close to covering the hassle, it seemed as if it might not be practical for Amelia to get out even that often, but it turned out not to be that bad.

"We can cope," Merlyn said, as the day of Lisa's birth approached. "I'm sorry that you've had to give up school, and I certainly want you to have every opportunity to complete your A levels at the tech, so I shan't expect or allow you to be skivvying night and day, but we can cope. I've had practice, after all. We'll be all right, the three of us. We'll see it through."

* * * * * * *

The second time Amelia saw her dead mother was on the stroke of midnight on the night after she gave birth to Lisa. While the ward was temporarily quiet Faith walked right past the duty nurse, as bold as you please, and came to stand beside Amelia's bed, looking down at the six-hours-old Lisa asleep in her crib.

"Really rips the guts out of you, doesn't it?" her mother said, undiplomatically. "I was heaving for hours. The pethidine kept wearing off, but women don't go in for midwifery unless they're accomplished sadists. That's why there are so few female serial killers—our demonic sisters get more and better kicks from supervising births than Hannibal Lecter will ever get from butchery."

"If you've come to say *I told you so*," Amelia began, "you can...."

"I haven't," Faith assured her. "I've come to warn you. That's what apparitions of the dead are supposed to be for, after all. The first time's just to let you know that we're around, to keep you on your toes. The second time's to tell you that you're going to need to be strong if you intend to see it through."

"And the third time?" Amelia asked, knowing that everything determined by legend and superstition happens in threes—especially misfortunes.

"We'll get to that," her mother said, darkly. "Let's not get ahead of ourselves. She lifted a hand to smooth her soft

105

hair, and Amelia noticed that her nail varnish was slightly chipped.

"What's it like?" Amelia asked.

"What's *what* like?" Faith countered, although she must have known.

"Being dead."

"It's not *like* anything. It just *is*. It's not Heaven, it's not the Underworld and it's not the Other Side. Dead is dead. The atoms of your body are scattered on the wind and dissolved in the earth, breathed in and out or bound into weeds and grime; the reality of what you were is dispersed into the memories of everyone who knew you, neglected and forgotten by almost everyone."

"Not Dad," said Amelia, knowing that it would be superfluous to mention herself. "He remembers. He's still mourning."

"That man was born to mourn," said Faith, cruelly. "Your little family will suit him right down to the ground. Lisa will mop up what little time for thought and space for feeling he has left. He'll be far too good to you, in the saintliest way imaginable, and he'll be a real wizard with the housework. You mustn't let that kind of life consume you, and you mustn't think you owe him anything extra because of it. You inherited far too much from me as it is—you mustn't think of your father as part of the package. You can still be a contender, if you put your mind to it. It's just a matter of trying that little bit harder."

"That's the warning, is it?" Amelia asked, contemptuously. "Don't let Dad become too dependent? Put more effort into building a career?"

"Don't get smart with me, Millie," her mother retorted, still too dignified even in death to call her a bloody stupid cow. "I'm the one who knows what I'm talking about. Death has its privileges. I've been where you are, remember, and I know what comes after it. I know the risks. I'm warning you that it's a lot easier than you think to go to your grave without ever having lived at all, and all it takes is inertia. I'm warning you that people who sit around waiting for the future to arrive always miss the bus. I'm warning you that people who spend their lives in the back seats of other people's cars never learn to drive. I'm warning you that people who pay too much attention to understanding the fundamental concepts without ever bothering to tighten up their calculations always get the answers wrong."

"I think you mean *silly little buggers* rather than people, Mum," said Amelia, helpfully.

"I know what I mean," said Faith Curtinshaw, ominously.

"Sure," said Amelia. "You're the one who's dead, after all. Can you really see into the future?"

"Of course I can't, you silly, silly girl. That's exactly what I'm trying to tell you. Nobody can, because you have to *make* the future. If you just let it happen, it never arrives."

"And that's what you think of your life, is it? You hung around with Dad and me, waiting for a future that never arrived, and you resent it like hell?"

Amelia would have understood if her mother had just turned around and walked away at that point, but she didn't. Instead, Faith went to the crib to look down at the sleeping Lisa. "All you inherit," she whispered, not to her daughter but to her granddaughter, "is the risk. Play your cards cleverly enough, and you can still win, even against the odds."

"She can't hear you," Amelia whispered, "and even if she could, she wouldn't understand."

Faith left then, without a backward glance, not needing to add the observation that the kid wasn't alone in not being able hear the voices of the dead or to understand their warnings—and would never find herself lacking in that kind of company.

* * * * * * *

As Amelia had anticipated, Merlyn Curtinshaw was a bloody good grandfather, hardly less than perfect. He looked after Lisa while Amelia went to evening classes at the tech to complete her A level courses in English, History and French. He looked after Lisa when Amelia went out with friends, of either sex. He needed no looking after himself, never giving the slightest hint that he was in any way dependent on his daughter. He continued to discharge his duties at the school without the slightest hint of negligence. His pupils continued to nickname him "the wizard".

"You ought to think about your own future, you know," Amelia told her father, the day her A level results came through and opened up the possibility of a university place. "You mustn't sacrifice yourself for me. You could get married again if you wanted to, start another family of your own."

"Most people," said Merlyn Curtinshaw, "spend their entire lives trying to be something they're not and arrive somewhere they aren't. I'm one of the lucky ones. I always knew that if I aimed for the moon I'd never get off the ground. I calculated what I could actually achieve, and I went for that, and I got it. Yes, I was devastated when your mum died—but things don't have to last forever to be worthwhile. You and she were everything I ever needed, and I still have that. I'm not sacrificing anything."

Although he had no more ability to foresee the future than anyone else, it turned out that Amelia's father was right. He wasn't sacrificing his future on the altar of his daughter's needs and desires, because he had no future to sacrifice. Three days after Lisa's third birthday, he went to the doctor to obtain an opinion about a peculiar lump that had appeared on his left testicle and had finally become too big to ignore.

"You should have come to me sooner," said the doctor, before sending Merlyn Curtinshaw to hospital as a top priority emergency admission.

Three days later Merlyn emerged from the operating theatre one testicle short, and three days after that he started chemotherapy. The attention and treatment he received were wondrously rapid and efficient. It was, he gladly judged, enough to restore anyone's faith in the much-maligned National Health Service.

"It's called Hodgkin's disease," the unlucky man explained to his daughter. "It's uncommonly aggressive. There's no history of it in my immediate family—but my immediate family isn't large enough to constitute a representative statistical sample. We Curtinshaws have never been prolific breeders." Amelia did not remark that some few of his cells seemed to be doing their damnedest to make up for that lack of profligacy in no uncertain terms.

Amelia's mother had not reacted well to her chemotherapy, and had herself remarked that it was like having exceptionally bad PMT twenty-eight days a month. She had lost her smile and smooth complexion along with her hair, and had similarly remarked that if this was what death warmed up looked like it was no wonder that people tried to avoid the condition.

It was not until some time after the chemotherapy ended, and the death sentence had been confirmed, that Faith had begun to look slightly better again. As she had moved inexorably toward her end, buoyed up by morphine and the gradual if somewhat apologetic return of her hair, Amelia's mother had become more human again, more contented in her flesh, and more inclined to smile. Amelia had thought at the time that there was a certain irony in the fact that the defiant last stand of the art and science of medicine had only wrought havoc with the ghost in her mother's machine, while the acceptance of inevitability had allowed that ghost a brief resurrection of sorts.

Amelia didn't expect that things would be much different with her father, and to begin with they weren't. He lost his mask of composure along with his hair, and turned into a rottweiler in human form; had he had marking to do, any of the silly little buggers who got the answers wrong would have got zero marks—but he did not, of course, have any actual marking to do, so the only person who was marked, and left pointless, by the experience was Amelia. He spent a lot of time apologizing for his failures, and quite a lot weeping and grinding his teeth in wrath and frustration over the fact that however sorry he was, he simply could not avoid them.

After the chemotherapy ended, having failed to eliminate the rampaging crab, Amelia expected her father to recover a little of his old self, much as her mother had, but he never did. His hair did begin to grow again, after a fashion, and the morphine did ease his pain, but the process of becoming more human again did not gift to Merlyn Curtinshaw the least hint of contentment, nor any inclination to smile. He had always been a forgiving man, but forgiveness had somehow been cut out of him, and he was no longer able to forgive himself. The fact that he was entirely innocent of any sin made no difference to the relentlessness of his determination to bathe in blame.

"I'm so sorry," Merlyn said to Amelia, when she brought Lisa to the neatly-kept hospice where her father had elected to die. "I wanted so much to be with you, to see you through, to give you the support you needed. So bloody stupid of me not to have taken any notice of it sooner, so bloody stupid of me to wrap my feelings up inside, twist everything up into a knot, so bloody stupid."

"It's not your fault, Dad," she told him. "You don't get cancer because you're uptight—that's just an old wives' tale. It's a lottery. It can happen to anyone."

She was being generous, of course. For herself and Lisa she was frightened half to death. Both of the generative organs from which she had been conceived had now proven rotten. She was the inheritor of a double curse, and she just had to hope that Jason Stringer's genes would prove to be made of sterner stuff. His parents were stern enough—Jason's mum refused to speak to her if they happened to pass one another in the aisles at Sainsbury's and Jason's dad had told her father (unnecessarily, given Merlyn's dislike of fuss and bother) that his boy wouldn't pay a penny in child support, even if the CSA sent the debt collectors round.

"You need me," Amelia's father insisted. "You need me, and I'm letting you down. Your mother told me to look after you, told me she'd haunt me if I didn't, and I'm letting her down."

"Did she haunt you?" Amelia asked, letting a little of her own anger show through. "Did she? Of course she didn't. First of all, because you did look after me, and second of all because you're a bloody scientist and you don't believe in bloody ghosts."

"That's not the point, Millie" he told her, mustering the last vestiges of his best schoolmasterish manner. "She didn't have to mean it literally. All she meant was that I inherited her responsibility along with mine, that I had two people's jobs to do instead of just one, and that I had to do it right because there was no one else to do it if I let you down. And I have."

"No you haven't," aid Amelia, firmly. "So shut up and smile. Shut up for Lisa, and smile for Lisa. Just because you're dying doesn't mean you have a right to frighten your granddaughter."

He tried, but he just couldn't do it. Even if he had contrived a smile, Lisa would probably have cried anyway, but he couldn't—and that, Amelia thought, was sad. What was the point of morphine if it couldn't set you free?

* * * * * * *

The third and last time that Amelia saw her dead mother was the night of her father's funeral, when everyone had gone home. The funeral had been surprisingly well attended, given that nobody, except for Amelia, Lisa and the absent Faith, had ever *liked* Merlyn Curtinshaw. Even his parents had found it easier to respect him, and it was respect that had pulled in the crowds from his school. His colleagues were unanimous in declaring that they felt the highest respect for his abilities as a teacher and for the way he had coped with the tragedies in his life. Amelia would have preferred it if they hadn't pluralized the tragedy, thus implying that Lisa's birth and Faith's death were two of a kind, but they were teachers and had to be forgiven their narrowness of view.

Merlyn's headmaster gave the funeral oration, taking great care to give credit where it was due. Merlyn Curtinshaw had been a man who cared, he said: a man who was always careful to make sure that his pupils understood the fundamental concepts of science, never so petty as to penalize them for minor errors in calculation. Merlyn Curtinshaw had been a man who believed in serving the community, he said, a modest man who never sought fame or acclaim, a contented man who was satisfied to do what he could. Merlyn Curtinshaw's nickname was "the wizard", he said, and Merlyn Curtinshaw really had been a wizard in every meaningful sense of the term.

"Funerals are always farcical," Amelia's mother observed, when she presented herself at the foot of Amelia's bed, dead on the stroke of midnight. "Of all ceremonial occasions, they're the ones which best reveal the essential cruelty of humor. Take away the laughter, and what does comedy become? Death is Nature's best and worst joke, and it always leaves the audience rolling in the aisles, splitting their sides. Some people even howl. Not you, though. You have your father's dignity. I like that."

"Okay," said Amelia. "I misunderstood the warning. I admit it. It simply never occurred to me that Dad was going to keel over and die. I didn't take steps to free myself from dependency, and now I'm a little bit lost. Silly, silly Millie."

"He was insured," her mother pointed out. "You're the proud owner of a house with its mortgage paid off."

"And I'm a single mother only just out of her teens, whose chances of starting university in October now look a little bit thin. Have you any idea what professional childcare costs?"

"Of course I have. Just because I'm dead it doesn't mean I'm out of touch."

"So I've noticed," said Amelia, sarcastically. "I suppose Dad will be dropping in from time to time, to render his apologies if not to offer his excellent advice."

"Don't be silly. He's a scientist—he wouldn't be able to believe in himself. He had a hard enough job while he was alive; he's no chance now. And you can't rely on me to keep popping up every time you need something. Just because I'm dead it doesn't mean I'm at your beck and call for all eternity."

Amelia remembered then—-without ever having quite forgotten it—that things connected with legend and superstition tended to happen in threes, especially misfortunes, and that there was every possibility that she would never see her mother again.

"Okay," Amelia said. "The first time was just to let me know that you were still around and that I wasn't the only bright girl ever to fall into the miscalculation trap. The second time was to offer me warnings that I wouldn't quite grasp, and taunt me with the possibility that I might lose out on everything life has to offer. The third time has to be a crunch of some kind—so what's the punch-line, Mum? Do I wake up now?"

"You woke up a long time ago," said Faith Curtinshaw, softly. "Some might think that you woke up far too soon, in the darkness before the dawn. But that isn't the deepest darkness—that's just an old wives' tale. The deepest darkness is still to come, and always is. Fortunately, the stars aren't scheduled to go out for another eighteen billion years or so, so you have a little time in hand, and you're not alone."

She meant Lisa. She knew that she didn't count.

"That's it?" said Amelia. "That's that all I get? Tomorrow is another day. I can get that from *Gone with the Wind* or *The Little Book of Calm*. For that, I don't need visits from my dead mother."

"So why do you need visits from your dead mother?" said Faith, wrong-footing Amelia yet again. "You tell me, Millie."

And that, Amelia realized, was the win-or-lose, do-or-die, put-up-or-shut-up question. She paused for a long time before she said: "Because I'm scared. Because I'm absolutely bloody terrified, and because even though I know damn well you can't see the future or make things right, I feel that I'm entitled. At the end of the bloody day, I'm entitled."

"There you are then," said her dear and dead but undeparted mother. "Count yourself lucky. Not many people get what they think they're entitled to. Even fewer get what they are entitled to."

"You just can't resist being glib, can you?" Amelia complained.

"Can you?" her mother countered.

Glib is good, Amelia thought, although she wasn't about to give her mother the satisfaction of hearing her concede the point. *Glib works. At least, it works a hell of a lot better than greed.* "It's not going to be easy, is it?" she said, aloud.

"No," her mother agreed. "That's the family curse. It never is easy, but you have to do it anyway. You have to try not to be silly, and you have to try to take charge. If you can make the best of what you have, you win the game. Even

113

Merl understood that, although his idea of winning wasn't necessarily mine—or yours. You haven't lost, Millie. You haven't even given the rest of the field that much of a start. You've stopped being a silly girl and you've moved from the back seat to the front, but now you have to start moving up through the gears. You won't find *Per Ardua ad Astra* in *The Little Book of Calm*—or *Gone with the Wind*, for that matter."

"Dad told me that his father was a Vauxhall man," Amelia remarked, glibly.

"Through and through," Faith agreed. "Through and through."

And that, as it turned out, was all the punch-line Amelia got, at least from her dead mother.

* * * * * **

"Who was that woman you were talking to last night?" Lisa asked Amelia, when they sat down to breakfast the next day. "I thought everyone had gone home."

"Did I keep you awake?" Amelia asked, more concerned about that than the arguably startling fact that Lisa had been able to eavesdrop on her apparition.

"I was awake anyway," Lisa said, delicately dipping a soldier in a soft-boiled egg. "I couldn't sleep. But I didn't cry. I don't, any more." She didn't mean that she never cried at all, only that she didn't cry just because she couldn't sleep.

"No," said Amelia, "you don't. I'd noticed that."

"So who was she?"

"Someone who came to help."

"With the funeral?"

"Yes—with the funeral. Lots of people helped. Grandma Curtinshaw and Granddad Booth—and the headmaster, of course."

"I don't have any grandmas or granddads any more," Lisa observed. Being a wise child, she didn't count the elder Stringers.

"You can share mine," Amelia assured her. "I've only got two left, I'm afraid. Most people my age still have all four, nowadays, not to mention a few extras roped in by divorce and remarriage, but you don't really need a crowd." She didn't start adding up parents, lest her further reassurances should sound ever so slightly hollow.

"The headmaster said that Granddad was a wizard," Lisa observed, "but he wasn't, was he?"

Amelia did not feel competent to explain the meaning of the word *metaphor* to a not-quite-four year old, so she simply said "No, he was a scientist. That meant he knew a lot, like wizards were once supposed to, but what he knew was mostly true."

"Was Grandma Faith a scientist too?" Lisa asked, looking up from under her eyebrows with a speculative expression which suggested that she had somehow guessed—impossible as it might be—exactly who Amelia had been talking to the night before. Fortunately, she also had egg-yolk wandering down her tiny chin, so her accusative manner had a hint of the farcical about it.

"No," said Amelia. "*Everything* Grandma Faith knew was true, and she never let you bloody forget it, either."

Lisa did not react to the swear-word; she already knew that hers was a family in which curses were not forbidden, provided only that they were used with discretion.

"The thing is," Amelia added, almost as if she'd been asked, "I'm almost exactly like her. Through and through. It might be the death of me, one day—but we'll just have to take the risk." Amelia tried for a second or two to forge a silent additional sentence which would glibly make use of the image of a spectre hanging over her, but the form of the words just wouldn't become clear so she gave it up. She hadn't the time to waste, she thought, and what did it matter anyway? "What you and I are going to be, my girl," she said, instead, as she wiped away the stray yolk, "is *contenders*."

THE WILL

He had always been able to make her do whatever he wanted.

If it had not been for that, Helen would not have returned—not even for his funeral; not even to hear the reading of his will. But he would have wanted her there, and she knew it. She hadn't needed the solicitor's letter, or the plea which Aunt Judith had sobbed down the phone; all that it took was the knowledge that he wanted her there. He hadn't wanted her there in some time—not for ten years—and while he hadn't wanted her, she hadn't gone, even though the house was still in some abstract sense her home; even though he was her father.

She didn't go to the house first, but to the funeral parlor where his body was laid in its coffin. They could be together there, just the two of them, both of them in their best suits.

He looked thinner, his skin discolored despite the best efforts of the embalmer. His mottled hands were shriveled, less hairy. She didn't touch him, and even though there was no one to observe she remained impassive and expressionless. She didn't shed a tear.

She shed no tears at the graveside, either, and there was no doubt that it didn't go unnoticed there.

Judith cried, of course, for the departed brother whose housekeeper and nurse she had become; but Judith was one of life's criers. The cousins wept a little too, but not for their uncle—their tears were sympathy tears for their mother, exhibitionist tears. Colin and Clare were paragons of a kind of showy sympathy which might easily pass for virtue.

Helen's brother, Michael, could not hold out in the face of their example; like the dutiful son he was he managed a dampened eye to set off his miserable face. But Helen was immune to all moral pressure; she simply stood, and listened.

She could imagine, all too readily, what the others thought of her performance.

Why did she even come?...frigid bitch...is that dark grey the nearest thing to black she could find?...not a hair out of place...face like a plastic doll...always his favorite, though... where was she when he was ill?...never came near the place...always his favorite...doesn't look a day over twenty-one...not one day older than the day she left...but it's all make-up, all fake...so thin...wouldn't surprise me if she were anorexic...frigid bitch....

Afterwards, though, they tried after their fashion to be kind. Judith did, anyhow. The cousins only put on a show of trying to be kind. The show, of course, was far more extravagant than the real attempt: "Mother did everything for him, you know...worked her fingers to the bone...wasn't easy...not his fault, of course, but he wasn't the most reasonable man in the world, once he fell ill...terrible thing, cancer...eating him up from the inside...not very nice for mother...."

Undoubtedly, they were right. Not very nice for mother. Not very nice for Saint Judith. Not as if the old man understood the meaning of gratitude.

"Of course we understand...your career...not very easy for you...half a day's drive from London...so busy...but you'll be too old for it soon, won't you...can't last forever...."

A sarcastic little thing, Clare, loud in her airing of unspoken questions. Where had Helen been? Where had Helen been, through all those years? Why wasn't it Helen who looked after the filthy old man, cleaning up after the thing which was eating him away inside?

Michael hardly had a word to say to her. He had always been a master of inarticulacy; he had learned to wear his silence well. People liked him for it. Judith fluttered round him when they all got back to the house—not like a moth around a flame, more like a mother hen working out some excess of maternal feeling in compulsive clucking. She fluttered round the vicar, too, as though trying to draw strength from whatever authority he had to deal with the aftermath of death. But such authority as he had was the authority of habit; he did this all too often, it was part of his way of life.

"I'm sorry," said a neighbor, conscientiously intruding upon Helen's isolation. "We were all very sorry. But he didn't suffer much. Morphine, you know. It must be ages since we saw you...are you famous now?"

"Ten years," said Helen, baldly. "It's been ten years."

"Such a long way from London," said the neighbor. "In the sticks."

That was the longest conversation she had. She froze them all out, one by one.

Frigid bitch.

Once, she could almost have sworn that she had heard the words spoken, but when she turned to stare at Colin and Clare, they weren't even looking in her direction.

The reading of the will seemed to Helen a complete absurdity. She had never thought of the reading of a will as something that was actually done in real life; the idea seemed to her so essentially theatrical that it ought surely to be confined to the screenplays of old films, where it could be used to determine who might be murdered. There had been no reading of a will when her mother had died, shortly before Helen had left home. Presumably her mother had left no will; she hadn't, after all, left a note.

When the family actually gathered around the dining table, with the owl-eyed solicitor at its head, the day's events seemed to Helen to have strayed into the realm of the surreal. She found it hard to focus her attention on what the little man was reading; his slow, punctilious manner of delivery was not conducive to concentration.

...To Michael, the bulk of the stocks and shares...to Judith, the sum of five thousand pounds....

Colin and Clare, seated one on either side of their saintly mother, seemed rigid with outrage when that was read out. Not that they had expected anything for themselves, of course, but for their mother...five thousand pounds, after all those years...only right, no doubt, that Michael should inherit the old man's investments, but the house...surely Judith deserved the house....

"...And to my daughter Helen," the solicitor read, in a voice like the creaking of old attic timbers, "the remainder of my estate, and all my love."

He coughed, then, in a disapproving manner, to show that the final phrase had been none of his doing, and did not really belong where the old man must stubbornly have insisted that it should be put.

The remainder of my estate....
...and all my love....

Colin and Clare were staring at her, wishing that she might be struck down, begrudging her the love as much as the house, because they were both unearned income, both undeserved reward. Clare's eyes were light blue, capable of an iciness that was barely imaginable.

There was more for the solicitor to say...about probate, about death duties...estimated time-scales, estimated amounts. The figures drifted by her, almost unheard. The house...worth a hundred and fifty thousand...twenty or thirty thousand on top of that...would she want to keep the house, or sell?...not rich, by today's standards, but *well off*...comfortable....

"Of course," St. Judith was saying to Michael, "I didn't expect him to think of me at all. You're his children, after all, and he was very kind to me after the divorce...he gave me a home...I don't think of it as payment for looking after him...I didn't expect any payment...it's just a small gesture of kindness...five thousand pounds...."

Michael murmured something in reply, retreating from her fluttering presence, looking at the floor, finding himself frustratingly cornered.

"You won't live here, of course," said Clare to Helen, in a challenging tone. "You live in London, now...when you're not traveling."

"I don't know," she replied, distantly. "Too early to make plans."

"But it's mother's home," said Clare, with an edge of aggression in her voice. "She's lived here for ten years. Ten years."

"Excuse me," said Helen, turning away from the icy eyes. She crossed the room to the corner where Michael was trapped, and touched Judith's arm. "Where am I to sleep?" she asked. "My things are still in the car."

"Oh, I'm sorry," said Judith, dabbing her bosom with her fingers as though performing some peculiar ritual of penance. "In your old room, of course. The attic room...I thought...will it be...?"

"That's fine," said Helen, "that's fine."

But when she had taken her case up to the room she came away again, immediately. She wasn't ready for it yet; even a long-drawn-out confrontation with the family, with the cousins she loathed and the brother she couldn't love, was something that could be endured...passed through...by way of delay.

It wasn't too difficult, even in the quiet hours after dinner, when Judith sought the comfort of the television...all the programs she didn't like to miss. Helen remained quite calm—impassive, inviolable. Nothing that was said got through to her, all enquiries were turned away, all conversational gambits squashed. What they thought of it, she didn't care. If it made them all uncomfortable to think that this was her house now, all the better. If envy were eating them up inside, the way cancer had eaten up the old man's flesh, then let it eat away. It was no concern of hers, nor any part of her purpose to soothe their anxieties, to try to make things right.

He wouldn't have wanted that.

He didn't want it.

That wasn't what he wanted at all.

When she finally went up to bed, and switched on the light, it all slipped out of her mind, and was gone. Instead, there was the room, just as it had been ten years ago: the red patterned carpet; the flowered wallpaper; the slanting ceiling; the neat bed with its polished wooden headboard; the posters blu-tacked to the wall; the dressing-table. Even the counterpane was the same. Why not? No one had slept here for ten years; there had never been any occasion to change anything, to buy anything new. Judith had come in to clean, week by week, but had moved nothing, had disturbed nothing, had wanted nothing from this part of the house.

Helen opened one of the drawers in the dressing-table, unable to remember what she would see, but knowing that when she looked, the memory would come back, and she would know that nothing had been disturbed.

She was right.

She sighed, and flipped open the case which she had abandoned on the bed, removing her clothes, her make-up... everything.

She had to go downstairs to the bathroom, but it was a stair that led nowhere except to the attic room: her own private passage, to her own private life. She saw no one in the corridor below.

It was not until she had undressed for bed, and turned the covers back, that she looked into the far corner of the room—the most shadowed corner, where there was a green chair with very short legs: a nursing chair. She stared at the chair for more than a minute, then went over, and moved it to one side, to expose the corner of the carpet. She lifted back the corner to reveal the varnished floorboards beneath. There was no dust; Judith's vacuum-cleaner had seen to that.

Helen lifted the loose floorboard, and put her hand within, groping in the shadowed pit between two beams. She lifted out an old magazine, folded vertically to fit it to its hiding-place. Its pages, once smooth and glossy, were brittle now; it had grown old and desiccated, and the colors were mottled, like the skin on the back of the old man's withered hands. It was very old; though the cover bore no date it was at least twenty-five years out of date. It had lived in its hiding-place for twenty-three...undisturbed for more than ten. It was old, and dead, fit only to return to some former state.

Ashes to ashes...dust to dust. Had they said that at the graveside?

She turned the pages gingerly, looking at the pictures. Little girls looked back at her. Seven-year-olds with their bums to the camera, peeping over their shoulders; nine-year-olds dressed in bizarre parody of French cabaret dancers; twelve-year-olds with careless fingers toying with their crotches. Thirteen-year-olds, sucking.

She looked mostly at their eyes, discolored by the years, sometimes hollowed by darkening of the pages, sometimes softened and shadowed...but the faces were still doll-like, the

121

poses carefully maintained. Little models...future professionals...the apples of their fathers' eyes.

She folded the magazine, wrapped it inside the blouse which she had worn to the funeral, and put it in her case.

Then she lay down, wondering what to think about in order to avoid the shabby memories of the day. She tried to empty her mind, to drift off into unconsciousness.

She was on the brink of falling asleep when the rain began, drumming upon the roof. It was a sound she had not heard for ten years, but she had known it so well that she recognized it instantly, and was quick to perceive its subtleties: the lighter tapping of the drops which struck the window-pane, the rattling of the spring-green leaves of the wych-elm which grew to the height of the eaves.

She listened to the rain for some little while.

Although she was awake, the sound of the rain seemed to carry her into a kind of dream, in which she seemed to be in the kitchen, standing beside the ironing-board, smoothing the creases from a white sheet. Her mother—or was it Aunt Judith?—was in the armchair beside the Aga, speaking about something in a matter-of-fact drone, though the words made no impression on her mind. Her own face was flushed, and she knew that someone was behind her, although she was staring at the iron and could not turn to look him in the face. She felt his hands, moving over her buttocks, moving into the cleft between her legs, the hairs on the back of the hands tickling the tops of her thighs. She tried to remain perfectly still, to give no sign to the woman in the armchair that anything was happening; but the woman in the armchair noticed nothing—she just went on talking, murmurously, meaninglessly....

The dream dissolved as she forced herself wide awake.

She thought for a moment that there was someone in the room.

She was sweating. She was very conscious of the sweat standing on her skin, wetting her night-dress, and could not understand why. It was an experience she had had before, when overheated by too many blankets, and she remembered now that she had sometimes woken up to a fleeting moment's alarm lest the house should be on fire, and she trapped beneath the eaves, with that private stair blocked by sheets of flame.

Often, when she was a child, she had extended a hand from the bed, leaning down to touch the floor, reassuring herself that the heat was only in her and not in the room. This time, though, she remained quite still. She knew that there was no fire consuming the floorboards from below.

The dream was no longer sharp in her mind, though it had not faded beyond recall. The feelings associated with the dream persisted; she was wettest of all between her legs. She could feel the sweat on her face forming into tiny droplets, and knew that her cheeks must be very red—though that was wrong, because she always used a pale foundation, and never blushed.

She had opened her eyes to stare into the darkness, and the room was briefly illuminated by a distant flicker of lightning. The storm was over the hills to the west, and the thunder which followed long after was a mere groaning in the wind, though some kind of echo of it seemed to ripple inside her, ascending into her viscera like a warm wave.

I'm ill, she thought. *These are symptoms of disease.*

Images of an ambulance-ride flickered through her mind, followed by images of herself lying awake upon an operating-table while a green-masked surgeon cut into her belly with a scalpel, and slipped a rubber-gloved hand into her abdomen, searching for something inflamed, something which was radiating heat.

The telephone's downstairs, she thought. *I can't reach it. Am I going to die here?*

She lay perfectly still, trying not to tempt the disturbance within her, thinking about appendicitis, wondering what it felt like when a cancer in the body first announced its presence in theatrical flourishes of mocking pain.

She hoped that the lightning would not cut the night in two again; she did not think that she could bear the thunder.

Her throat felt dry, and she swallowed, uncertain now whether she really felt pain, or whether it was only a dream that had bathed her in heat, in imaginary fire. She had always had such dreams, but had never burned...But she did not normally sweat like this, had never sweated like this before... had she?

It was very dark outside, but the window was not curtained, and enough light came in to crowd the room with misshapen shadows, which seemed as her eyes struggled to make sense of them to be moving.

Something seemed to be moving inside her, too, more insistent than a ripple or a wave...not sharp, like the surgeon's knife, but solid.

I'm possessed, she thought. *There's something taking possession of me...a demon made of darkness.*

Then the lightning lit up the room again, a little more brightly this time, and she saw all at once that the attic was quite empty of any other human presence. There was no one in the room. She was still puzzling over this when the thunder came, rumbling over the far-off hills.

Her legs, which had been closed tightly together, were prised apart. The sweat-sodden material of her night-dress clung briefly to the flesh of her thighs, and then rode up, exposing her crotch to the touch of cool, clean cotton. For a moment, the coolness was a welcome relief, but then the cold began to move up inside her, as the heat formerly had, like a shaft of ice sliding into her belly.

She opened her mouth to cry out, but no sound came because her throat was suddenly gripped by an insistent constriction that was neither cold nor hot, but terribly tight. A weight seemed to be upon her, pressing her back into the soft mattress, and she felt that something foul and dangerous was inside her, drawing her deeper into herself, as though there were a vacuum in her heart, and she collapsing about it, imploding.

What does it feel like, she asked herself, *when your appendix bursts? How long does it take you to die?*

She was surprised that she was still so completely conscious. She seemed to be too keenly aware of everything that was around her, everything that was inside her. She was thinking too quickly. The coldness was gone now, but there was still something inside her, stirring her as if it were a liquid tide, ebbing and flowing, much slower than her heartbeat. She felt that she had to get away from it if she could, and suddenly squeezed her eyes tightly shut, thinking that if only she could close herself off the demon might be expelled, forced out, exorcised. If only she could rescind her faith in demons, she thought, she would be safe from their assaults...if only she could cease to believe....

But when the lightning flashed again, she realized that her eyes were not shut at all, that she had opened them again even though she had fought so hard to shut them.

The wych-elm in the garden shook its emerging leaves in response to the cruel wind, yammering and chuckling, as though some idiotic night-hag had perched herself beneath the lintel of the window, to delight in her predicament.

Helen suddenly arched her back as the thunder seized her, consuming her senses with its throaty roar, and instead of imploding about her vacuous heart she was suddenly taut inside her skin, straining at the boundaries of her flesh.

She managed to cry out at last, but it was only a tiny whimper—as meager a sound of protest or pain as anyone could ever have imagined.

The rain laughed as it pelted the window-pane; but then the wind veered, or died, and the wych-elm slowed in the paces of its madcap dance, released by the force which had driven it.

Minutes passed, languorously, painlessly.

The sweat began to feel cool upon her skin. It began to go away...soaked up, perhaps, by the cotton sheet. She was able to turn upon her side, and knew now that she was not ill, was not dying. She knew that the visitor had gone, and left her to wait until the day she went to hell, before she burned in earnest.

She drew her thin knees up towards her tiny breasts, assuming a quasi-fetal huddle, comfortable in her self-enclosure.

When she was completely calm again, she drifted back into that state between sleep and wakefulness where daydreams could turn into real dreams, and at last she began to go over in her mind the events of the day.

She remembered the graveside, and began to weep, very quietly, and very gently. She remembered the grotesqueries of the funeral party, the bizarre reading of the will.

The Haunted Bookshop, by Brian Stableford

To my daughter Helen, the remainder of my estate...
...and all my love....

It was her heritage, and it really did not matter in the least whether she lived in the house, or in London...or whether she sold the house, or simply abandoned it to the dutiful care of St. Judith. None of that mattered...not any more.

Her father had worked it all out.

He had always been able to make her do whatever he wanted.

Always.

The Haunted Bookshop, by Brian Stableford

DANNY'S INFERNO

Shortly after my eleventh birthday my best friend, Danny Gearey, was stabbed to death in a playground fight that he hadn't started but had begun to look as if he might win. The funeral service was awful, although I was let off reading the silly poem because Beatrice Mews wanted to do it, and everyone agreed that she had a much better voice. I was glad to get out into the fresh air, although the sky was grey and I expected it to start raining at any moment. I didn't know what they'd do if it did start to rain and the grave started to fill up with muddy water. The coffin was made of wood, and Danny hadn't weighed all that much, so I figured that it would probably float—which would have seemed a little odd, all things considered.

I was surprised when I saw Danny lurking behind one of the older gravestones, not just because—unlike some I could name—he wasn't the kind of person you'd expect to turn up at his own funeral, but because he didn't look a day over seven and a half.

I slipped away to ask him how things were going now that he was dead.

"Not great," he admitted.

"Jez got expelled," I told him. Jez was the boy who'd stabbed him.

"I know," he said, hitching up his short trousers. His clothes were a bit Sunday-bestish, and surprisingly clean considering that he was leaning on a filthy tombstone. I guessed that dirt doesn't stick to the dead as easily as it sticks to the living.

"It served him right," I said. "Can anyone else see you, or is it just me?"

127

"Anyone can see the dead if they bother to look, but no one does. The living are good at not looking, but you tend to lose the knack when you die, and it's really difficult getting it back." He seemed to be loosening up a bit, although he hadn't said that he was glad to see me. Perhaps he'd been seeing me for some time, and was annoyed that this was the first time I'd been able to return the favor.

"I've never seen anyone else who's dead," I told him, defensively. "This is a first. Must be because we were best friends."

"I doubt it," he said. "The people who knew you best are the least likely to look, so rumor has it. Mind you, I haven't been here very long, so they might be winding me up. You know how it is when you're the new boy. It was probably just a freak of chance that made you look. You always were a bit freaky."

I didn't take offence; part of being best friends is being allowed to say that sort of thing one another, safe in the assumption that it'll be taken as a joke. "How come you've gone back to being seven?" I asked.

"I'm in Hell," he told me. "In Hell, everyone is the age they were when they'd committed enough sins to be irredeemably damned. Seven's quite old, actually."

"You got the day off, though?" I said. "To go to your funeral, I suppose."

"You don't get days off in Hell," he said, more tiredly than scornfully. "Hell is right here, just like Heaven and Earth. It's all one place, but we hardly ever bump into one another, even though the living can't see the dead. The same sixth sense that allows the living not to look allows them not to listen and not to touch as well."

I reached out and prodded him in the chest. He and his white button-up shirt were quite solid, even though the middle of his chest was three inches lower down than when I'd last prodded him. He didn't prod me back.

"Can you see the people in Heaven?" I asked.

"Sure," he said, "Although I'm trying to learn not to look. They all look exactly as they did when they died, and they're mostly very old. It's not true what they say about the good dying young. The good are unobtrusive. They don't take risks, so they mostly live to a ripe old age."

"Are they happy in Heaven?" I asked, although it seemed a silly question even at the time.

"Very," he said.

"What about all the kids who died before their burden of sin got to the pass mark for Hell?" I asked, anxious to make up for the previous question with one that would show that I was thinking hard about what he was telling me. "Must be lots of them."

"There aren't," he said. "Some think there might be another place, but most say that's just a myth, and others reckon that they have to retake the exam, and get recycled somehow."

People sometimes think I'm not too bright, but Danny was nearer to the mark when he called me a bit of a freak. My brain works fine, just not the way that my parents and teachers seem to want it to. I could see the logic of what he was saying, and I still wanted to impress him with my ability to learn something from this unexpected opportunity.

"So none of the dead is in what you might call the prime of life?" I said—but realized immediately that I'd put it entirely the wrong way and hastened to make up for it. "What I mean," I added, "is that the way to tell it, the prime of death seems to be ninety-nine with galloping Alzheimer's—but blissful."

"I couldn't put it that way myself," he said. "There are some dead people of working age, though—and that's mostly what they do."

"Work, you mean?"

"Yes. Mostly they look after the rest of us, so they're in Heaven as well as Hell, and sometimes both at the same time. Some call that purgatory, but others think they're not ex-living people at all, but something else. They don't seem entirely certain themselves."

"You mean they're angels and demons—or both, rolled into one?"

"Maybe."

"So it's not really that different from being alive," I said, trying hard to keep abreast of the news. "Hell sounds to me to be more of an eternal bore than a place of torment, and even Heaven doesn't sound as if it's worth the price of admission."

Danny looked away, slightly embarrassed. "You have to remember that I haven't been here that long," he muttered. "Since I never actually got the chance to grow up, I'm not sure how the others feel about what they've lost. Ten to seven's not a big step back, and I can't really imagine what being grown up would have been like. From here, it doesn't seem that much fun. Either way, though, I'm not really in a position to make sound comparisons. Sorry if I've given you the wrong idea."

In another conversation it might have been time to change the subject, but when you're face to face with your dead best friend in the middle of his funeral, it doesn't seem very fitting to talk about homework or football. "I suppose if no one ever looks at you, you can go pretty much where you want," I said. "See pretty much whatever you want—even nick pretty much what you want."

"We don't steal," he said.

"I suppose not," I said, realizing that the living would notice things going missing if the dead spent all their time pilfering. "I suppose nicking becomes a bit pointless if there's nothing you need."

"That's not the reason," he told me. "The dead can't commit sins. The Heaven crowd don't want to, of course, but we just can't—it's not in our nature any more. So no, I can't go wherever I want or see whatever I want, let alone nick whatever I fancy. As I say, I'm trying to learn not to look. It's easier that way—the living don't know how lucky they are to be so good at it."

"I do now," I said. "You've just told me. Will I be able to see you again, do you think? And all the other dead people?"

"Do you see any other dead people around?" he asked.

"I don't know," I said. "I see plenty of people—how do I know which of them are dead and which are alive?"

"If they're mostly adults, they're probably alive," he reminded me. "Actually, this place is pretty crowded. Cemeteries usually are. You're pretty good at the not looking lark, even though you caught sight of me. Maybe you'll see me again, maybe you won't. Don't try, though—trying doesn't help. It's the opposite of trying not to think of a pink elephant, and just as difficult."

"Did you hear Beatrice Mews read that poem in the church," I asked, "or are churches off-limits to people in Hell?"

"No and no. Churches aren't off-limits, but I waited out here and missed the poem. Was it any good?"

"Total crap. She was just showing off. You know what she's like—any excuse."

"You might want to watch that sort of thinking," Danny said. "If, by some freak of chance, you're not already irredeemably damned, even a little thing like that might push you over the edge."

"I didn't do anything!" I protested.

"You might be surprised how little it takes," he told me. "On the other hand, it's probably too late to start worrying about it now. I shouldn't have mentioned it. You'll probably end up seven, just like me—except that you were a little taller, as I recall."

As I recalled, he'd have been far more likely to say "fatter and uglier" when he was alive, but he was incapable of sin now—not that it had prevented him referring to me as "a bit freaky". Perhaps, I thought, "freaky" wasn't reckoned an insult by the powers that be.

That thought made me realize that there were other sorts of question I ought to be investigating. "Have you seen God?" I asked.

"No," he replied. "A privilege reserved for the pure in heart, apparently."

"Not exactly a long queue, then," I said, wondering if wit might be intrinsically sinful, even at that feeble level.

"So rumor has it," he agreed. "It's probably true, give that envy and spite are among the knacks we've lost, along with not looking."

"Still," I said, "your kind of Hell must be better than lakes of boiling blood and all that."

"Oh yes," he said, in a tone that seemed deadly in its neutrality. "There's lots to be grateful for."

THE HAUNTED BOOKSHOP, BY BRIAN STABLEFORD

"And some day," I said, "we'll probably be together again—seven-year-olds united in friendship, for ever and ever. Something to look forward to." I was, of course, thinking of him looking forward to it rather than me. I was eleven now.

"Yeah," he said. "I'm trying to learn not to look, but I guess we'll always be glad to see one another, won't we?"

And then he vanished—just disappeared, like some kind of special effect.

It had just started to rain, but the vicar didn't stop reading—he just hurried along a little. I must have missed the bit about ashes to ashes and dust to dust. I went back to the graveside, and put my hand in Mum's, as if nothing had happened. She hadn't noticed that I'd gone. Nobody had, even though the living are much better at keeping an eye on one another than they are at seeing the dead. It must have been Danny's presence that allowed me to go unnoticed for a few minutes, because things went back to normal as soon as I touched Mum's hand, and she's certainly kept an eye on me since then. She says it's because she has to be extra careful now she knows that kids aren't safe even in a school playground, but it might be that the living have to concentrate that much harder to one another in order to avoid seeing the dead.

I told Mum what had happened, of course, and Dad too—and quite a few other people. I even told Beatrice Mews. They didn't listen. They probably wouldn't have believed me if they had, but it never came to that, because they didn't hear what I said, no matter how many times I tried to tell them. I guess I caught a glimpse of what it's like to be dead in more ways than one...my destiny, I suppose, if I'm not completely bonkers.

I don't think I'm completely bonkers, or even that I was temporarily bonkers because I was at my best friend's funeral. A bit freaky, maybe, but not completely bonkers. I never saw Danny again after that day, but I don't know whether that was because I was trying too hard to look, or not trying hard enough. It affected me, though, having that little chat. I think about Danny every time I do something wrong, not because I worry about the wrong thing being the one that finally brings my sin tally to damnation level—I figure that if Danny got there three years before he died, it would need a miracle for my fate still to be hanging in the balance—but because I can't help feeling slightly grateful to be able to do wrong at all. While I'm alive, I'll always have that privilege, and the thought that it will be something I'll lose after I die makes me appreciate it in a way I never did before the day of Danny's funeral.

That's why I thought it might be a good idea to write this down, for the benefit of others, although I don't suppose that anyone will ever read it.

THE HAUNTED BOOKSHOP, BY BRIAN STABLEFORD

CAN'T LIVE WITHOUT YOU

It started quietly, with dark and silent calls on the videophone in her room at the nurses' home. At first, Pris just said hello a few times, then cut the connection, but she eventually became impatient with herself for doing that. It seemed superfluous saying hello to a black screen twice or three times if the first one elicited no response. After calling him a sad bastard three times she got impatient with herself all over again, and resolved to be more inventive, but she ran out of synonyms for "sad bastard" sooner than she would have imagined possible. He never bothered to withhold the number from which he was calling, but he used public plug-ins located in the hospital complex, of which there were hundreds.

Pris decided not to worry about it. There were, after all, plenty of sad bastards in the world, and the hospital often seemed like a factory for turning out more. Pris worked on the cancer wards, and although she was always being told by the older hands that things were getting better every day as more and more new treatments came on line, the science always seemed to be one step behind the reality of suffering and death. Lots of patients got cured nowadays, but lots didn't. Lots was the operative word, because it really did seem like a lottery, and by comparison with what was happening every day on the wards a few funny phone calls didn't seem like anything to get worked up about.

Charlotte, who worked with Pris on the cancer wards and had the room next to hers in the nurses' home, didn't agree.

"It's your duty to report it," she said. "You have to report it to Human Resources, because at least some of the calls are coming from inside the hospital, and you have to report it to the police."

"Hospitals are stressful places," Pris said, uncertainly. "They disturb people. Nurses are bound to be the objects of the occasional fixation. The people we deal with day by day don't know whether they're going to live or die, and we're in the trenches with them while they're fighting for their lives. It sometimes makes it easier for them to reinterpret their anxiety as sexual attraction, but they know deep down that's what they're doing. They get confused. We have to expect the occasional crank call."

"But we don't have to tolerate it," Charlotte insisted. "This is the twenty-first century. There are laws against stalking now, and we have to use them. There are lines to be drawn, and we have to stick to them. There are far too many freaks about, and far too many of them still hang around nurses' homes, because they're obvious targets. We have to do our bit by way of self-defense."

In the end, they agreed to compromise. If it hadn't stopped by the end of the month, or if it escalated, then Pris would report it to Human Resources and the police.

It didn't stop, and it did escalate.

Hand-decorated cards started arriving in the post, and pictorial emails queued up to be downloaded to her home station and her palmtop. The first few designs were stylized hearts and hands, but the motifs evolved rapidly to become more and more like anatomical studies. There were faces too, sometimes cut away to reveal the muscles within. The sender began to add color, using felt-tipped pens and then acrylic paints on the actual cards. Red, not unnaturally, was always dominant. The images weren't particularly horrible—Pris had seen more gruesome illustrations while she was training, and she was a daily witness to far worse things on the wards—but they were definitely perverse, given their accompaniment by the messages scrawled inside the cards or displayed in exotic fonts on the electronic cartoons. The emails arrived via three different servers, all of them launched by unidentifiable mobile units of one kind or another.

THE HAUNTED BOOKSHOP, BY BRIAN STABLEFORD

The messages weren't threatening—they said things like LOVE YOU, PRIS and THINKING ABOUT YOU, and even CAN'T LIVE WITHOUT YOU—but they didn't seem to fit the drawings at all. There was never an I at the beginning of a message, but Pris figured that if the stalker were the kind of person who could put an I at the beginning of sentences like that he'd probably be the kind of person who'd introduce himself in the street, not the kind of person who'd make silent calls—except that the calls were no longer completely silent. Nowadays, he sometimes asked her if she'd got the latest card, and sometimes, if she let a silence develop after he spoke, he'd whisper whatever he'd written on the card in question, always without the I.

"Love you lots."

"Thinking about you, Pris."

"Can't live without you."

The pictures and the fact that he had begun to speak gave her a license to be more inventive in her replies. When he asked whether she'd got his latest she could say something like "Yes, and it was awful. Who do you think you are, Vincent van bloody Gogh?" and when he told her to have a nice day she'd say something like "I probably would if I wasn't being fucking *stalked*." When he said he couldn't live without her, though, puzzlement and a slight twinge of guilt always displaced anger. "But you are living without me," she'd point out. "You might be getting on my nerves a bit, but you're not living *with* me, are you? In fact, you don't seem to have much of a life at all. What's it all about, eh?"

Eventually, Pris confessed to Charlotte that things had got worse. Then she had no alternative but to honor her promise and report the calls, the emails and the cards to the relevant authorities.

Human Resources weren't interested. "This is a hospital," the young woman said. "It happens all the time. If you want to bring a specific complaint against a particular individual we'll carry it forward for you, but until then it isn't worth our while to fill out a form."

The police were less dismissive. A WPC Clarke called round to take a look at the cards and the locally-postmarked envelopes in which they had been delivered—but then the

THE HAUNTED BOOKSHOP, BY BRIAN STABLEFORD

WPC told Pris, glumly, that there wasn't a lot they could do under the provisions of the current law unless and until the stalker could be identified, and even then they wouldn't be able to charge him unless he made a real nuisance of himself, preferably by making threats of violence or employing graphic pornographic language.

"I don't suppose you have any idea who it might be?" the policewoman asked.

"Well, it's obviously somebody at the hospital, or someone who's been in the hospital," Pris said, having already given the matter a great deal of thought. "Patients do get funny ideas about nurses sometimes, but because they've already seen us and are used to talking to us they're more given to face-to-face embarrassment. With it being a big-time teaching hospital, though, there's no shortage of geeks around. When you add three hundred students, who are mostly male, and two hundred lab technicians, who are mostly male, to the junior doctors, who are mostly male, and then add in the nurses, porters, research scientists, cleaners, IT support staff and consultants, you're well into four figures—and that's not to mention the guinea pigs."

"Guinea pigs?" WPC Clarke queried.

"The volunteers who take part in experiments and clinical trials. The on-site researchers subcontract work from a lot of biotech and pharmaceutical companies. They're still working their way through the fallout of the Human Genome Project and the Human Proteome Project. They often run trials with anything up to a couple of hundred people in the experimental and control groups. A lot of the subjects are unemployed, earning extra spot cash—guinea-pigging fees aren't deductible from means-tested benefits, you see, because they're a kind of national service. It all adds up to a hell of a lot of potential suspects. The more paranoid I become the more I look around, but there are way too many screwballs lurking in every possible direction."

"I see," the policewoman said, sadly. "Unfortunately, all I can advise you to do for the moment is keep on looking. You can get BT to filter your calls and emails, if you want, and log the traces for you, just in case he gets careless. You ought to save all the cards and envelopes, however innocuous they are, so that they can be produced as evidence of an escalating obsession if things continue to get worse."

"Thanks," said Pris, feeling slightly guilty about having wasted police time because nothing WPC Clarke had told her had been unexpected. "Maybe they won't get worse. He hasn't made any threats, and he seems to be more interested in drawing hands and hearts than offensive parts of the anatomy."

"Actually," the policewoman said, looking at the designs on the cards, "they're not that bad. If he wasn't such a sad bastard, he might make an artist. Perhaps the practice will do him good."

"They're too clinical," Pris said. "That's not art. It's just third-rate reportage."

* * * * * * *

"The thing I worry about," Pris said to Charlotte, as they came off shift a couple of days later, "is the way he seems to be working towards a goal. First silent calls, then he speaks. First sketches, then all the colors of the rainbow, though admittedly mostly red. Where's it supposed to end up?"

"Up some dark alley with a butcher's knife," Charlotte said. "That's where it always ends."

"Only in the movies," Pris objected. "In real life, these things are mostly harmless. That's what Human Resources says. He doesn't seem to mean me any harm. Maybe he isn't working towards anything at all. Maybe he's just making progress away from something—gradually shedding inconvenient inhibitions."

"It's what he'll do when his inhibitions are gone that worries me," Charlotte said, although it wasn't evident to Pris that Charlotte needed to be worried at all. "He's probably one of those kids who grew up in solitary confinement with a PC and never got around to ordinary human communication. They always turn violent—it's all those games full of ray guns and big swords. Have you thought of getting Security to check the hospital CC-TV cameras to see if they can spot people making calls on their mobiles at the relevant times? Security are bound to be more helpful than Human Resources."

"It's a hospital," Pris reminded her. "Every corridor's full of people yammering into the public plug-ins all day and all night because they're not allowed to use battery-powered mobiles around sensitive equipment. If it is a patient, he'll either get better or die. At first I thought it was probably someone we'd discharged, but he's making too much use of widely-spaced hospital facilities. He doesn't use the same post-box all the time—and before you suggest sticking pins with colored heads into a map, I've tried it. It's more likely that he's staff. He knows so much about me that he's probably got access to the hospital directory. He probably lives locally too."

"He might be an out-patient or a regular at the testing centre."

"Out-patients and guinea pigs don't have access to the hospital directory," Pris pointed out.

"He might if he's a hacker," Charlotte said. "If he grew up in solitary with a PC, he's probably an expert hacker."

"You watch way too many movies," Pris told her. "Anyway, I've never tried to keep my personal details secret. My number and email addresses are available to anyone at the touch of a button, except that the directories only have my initial—not even Priscilla, let alone Pris. But he could have overheard someone calling me that on the ward, or in the canteen or the shop, or even in the street, without actually knowing me at all."

"The trouble is," Charlotte said, having long abandoned any responsibility she might have felt to be reassuring and supportive, "that we get more freaks passing through with every month that passes. Too many new drugs that mess with people's heads, sometimes in ways nobody suspects until they start on the trials. The guinea pigs have to pretend to be normal to get taken on, but that just means they're good at pretending. The people tabulating the results are just as weird, so far as I can tell. You'd think the pill-pushers would do it themselves, but no—they hire yet more losers and misfits to do it for them."

"They can't do it themselves," Pris said. "There has to be a double blind, or the expectations of the experimenters can skew the results almost as much as the placebo effect. Sometimes, I wonder if he might be some kind of experimenter, working through a program to find out what happens—with the final phase yet to begin."

"Well, I'm no tabulator" Charlotte said. "If he wants to find out how you're responding, he'll have to show himself eventually. When he does, give him an extra kick in the balls for me, will you? I feel that I'm losing out on all the conversations we might be having about me."

Whether there was an experimental program or not, the escalation continued. Six weeks after his first phone call Pris's stalker sent her what appeared to be a semen-stained handkerchief. She took it to the police station immediately.

"That's an offence, isn't it?" she said to WPC Clarke. "Sending obscene and noxious material through the post. Charlotte says that it's definitely against the law."

WPC Clarke confirmed that there was, indeed, a law to that effect, but that she would have to liaise with the Post Office's Internal Investigations Department for reasons of jurisdictional protocol. The man from the Post Office, whose name was Robertson, offered to arrange for all Pris's mail to be opened at the sorting office, thus intercepting any more obscene and noxious materials, but Pris couldn't see the point.

"You'll still have to tell me about them, won't you?" she said. "Even if you don't, he will, sad wanker that he is—and intercepting them won't get us any nearer to catching him."

"We take these matters very seriously," Mr. Robertson assured her. "We'll ask all our mail-collectors to be vigilant. The police lab will take a DNA-print off the handkerchief and check it against their database, although nothing will show up there if he hasn't got a criminal record. You might have better luck with the hospital's own data-base, if you can figure out a way round the Data Protection Act." He wasn't suggesting that she hire a hacker, of course—merely pointing out that the hospital must have its own internal investigation procedures. Unfortunately, there were problems of jurisdictional protocol there too; Human Resources and Security were equally anxious not to cross the blurred line that allegedly separated their areas of responsibility.

Human Resources told her—not unexpectedly—that confidential records couldn't be examined unless there was firm and specific proof of wrongdoing by a particular hospital employee, while Security contented themselves with complaining about what a bunch of prize arseholes Human Resources were, and how their hands were always tied when push came to shove.

The only substantial change in Pris's circumstances, in fact, was that Mr. Robertson came knocking on her door every time the people at the sorting office found what they considered to be a suspicious package with her address on it.

The first two were false alarms, but the third one wasn't. It was another semen-stained handkerchief, carefully wrapped around a neatly-severed ear.

* * * * * * *

"Well," said the Post Office investigator, as he took the ear away in order to deliver it to WPC Clarke, "if it isn't a fake you'll certainly know him if you see him. The police shouldn't have any trouble finding him now."

Pris began, rather belatedly, to regret the crack she'd once made about Vincent van bloody Gogh. She even apologized for it when the stalker called to ask whether she'd received the latest token of his esteem. "Look," she said, "you obviously need help. Sending messy packages to me isn't doing you any good, and it certainly isn't doing me any good. I understand that you're a troubled individual and I really do want to help you, because I'm a nurse and that's my job, but we have to re-think this whole business. Tell me who you are, and we'll sort it. Failing that, just tell me why you're doing it, and where it's all supposed to be leading. Self-mutilation is a serious business. This can't go on."

"Can't live without you, Pris," the stalker said. "Have a nice day."

Her temper snapped and she the told him in no uncertain terms that she didn't want any more gifts, that she didn't want anyone to be unable to live without her, and that she wouldn't have a single nice day until he stopped what he was doing for good and all.

"Love you, Pris," was his only response.

Unfortunately, Mr. Robertson's optimism proved to be premature. No matter how much looking around she did, she couldn't see anyone with a missing ear, and nor could the police.

"Actually," WPC Clarke told her, when the report came back from the police lab, "having looked at the ragged edge, they're pretty sure that it wasn't cut off a person at all. They think it was stripped from some kind of artificial substrate, having been grown *in vitro*. It's not such a giveaway as we'd hoped, but it narrows the field down quite a bit. We can probably concentrate our attentions on the hospital research labs. The ear's DNA matches the semen, which narrows the field even further. I'm going up there to ask a few questions."

Pris didn't have to ask the WPC to explain her logic. If the semen was the stalker's and the ear hadn't been cut off the wanker's head, then the ear must be cloned from some of his own tissue. Which meant that the stalker had to be involved, one way or another, in stem cell tissue-regeneration. Restoring multipotency, or even pluripotency, to differentiated cells, was one of the hottest prospects in contemporary medical research. The re-empowered cells could then be set up in glass wombs as quasiblastular entities, with the aim of redifferentiating them into organs, limbs or whatever, which could then be transplanted back into the tissue-donor without any rejection problems.

"There's a certain irony in it, isn't there?" Charlotte said, when Pris passed on the strange news. "I mean, the guy's obviously a social inadequate, impotent in any meaningful sense of the term, but he's also an expert on the restoration of multipotency to differentiated tissue. Overcompensation, or what?"

"He's not necessarily an expert on anything," Pris pointed out. "Statistically speaking, the tissue samples are far more likely to come from an experimental subject than an experimenter. The semen could have come from the hospital sperm bank. Probably did, in fact."

"No way," Charlotte opined. "It has to be the stalker's own produce. Where would the symbolism be if he'd just withdrawn it at random from the bank? You know what narcissists these tissue-culture cowboys are. They all use their own stuff in their tinker-toy outfits. He's probably got a whole shelf full of jars containing monster versions of his own pathetic prick."

That conjured up possibilities that Pris didn't really want to think about, although she supposed she ought to try, just in case. She was glad, now, that Mr. Robertson was always on hand to open her suspicious packages for her, even though she still felt obliged to be present when he did.

The next one was a hand.

The hand wouldn't have seemed half as bad if it had been fully grown, but it wasn't. It was tiny: the hand of a baby. But the baby in question had the same DNA as the semen, so it had to be a clone. WANT TO HOLD YOUR HAND was scrawled on the piece of paper in which the hand was wrapped.

"I don't get it," WPC Clarke said, when she reported the lab results back to Pris. "Why wasn't the ear tiny as well? He can't have been growing it for twenty years, can he?"

"Multipotent quasiblastular entities can grow a lot faster than whole individuals," Pris told her, "because they're only peripheral entities, without much organic complexity. I only got the outside part of the ear—the shape. I didn't get the internal bit that actually does the hearing. The hand probably grew in a matter of hours—if he'd waited a couple of days, it would have been full-sized, but it wouldn't have been able to grip, to feel, to work. It would have looked wrong, unreal. Don't you have any suspects yet?"

"None," the policeman reported, dolefully. "The evidence indicating that it's a doctor or lab worker rather than an experimental subject is too circumstantial to get us a warrant allowing us to run a match against the hospital's DNA database. Your Human Resources people told me that it probably wouldn't do any good even if we could, because the companies paying for that kind of research keep their own databases, under security seals so tight that no common-or-garden warrant could ever get us in. We can't even get a list of names of people involved in that kind of work at the hospital—the companies take the threat of industrial espionage very seriously."

Again, Pris decided to reason with the stalker the next time he called. "Okay," she said, "So you're too sensible to go in for self-mutilation, at least not in any ordinary sense of the word. That's good. That's healthy. We can work with that. I'm prepared to believe that a man who stops short of carving himself up, even when he wants to send bits of himself through the post, is also prepared to stop sort of carving me up, which is sort of reassuring. So, given that you probably don't want to hurt me, do you think you could possibly see your way clear to giving up trying to scare the hell out of me? It's not right."

"Mean you no harm," the stalker said. "Love you, Pris. Offer you my heart."

Pris felt that she knew her persecutor well enough by now to assume that the last remark wasn't metaphorical—and so it proved. The next suspicious package turned out to contain a full-sized heart, with the accompanying caption OFFER YOU MY HEART.

"Hearts are difficult," Pris explained to her two investigators, who were so fascinated by her case by now as to be neglecting their other work. "You need pluripotent stem cells to grow a functional heart, so anyone working exclusively with the multipotent variety is probably out of the frame. I don't think we need worry about the next step being a brain, or even an eye. No one's managed to grow anything that complicated yet. I looked it up in the hospital library."

"I don't understand the difference between all these different kinds of potency," WPC Clarke complained.

"The cells in an early embryo are totipotent—capable of becoming any kind of specialized cell at all," Pris explained. "As soon as differentiation sets in, though, the cells become pluripotent, with some possibilities already closed off. The potential continues to shrink. The stem cells retained in an adult body are only capable of developing into a few specialized types. That's multipotency."

Mr. Robertson was less interested in the technical details. "It makes you wonder what he'll think of next, though, doesn't it?" he said, thoughtfully.

Pris had to agree with that. The longer the process went on, the fewer ultimate objectives seemed to be likely, or even possible—but the ones that remained seemed quite ominous enough.

"He's a liar, whoever he is," WPC Clarke pointed out. "That's not really his heart. It's just a spare part, manufactured in a lab, probably botched like the hand, though not as obviously."

That, Pris thought, was the first useful insight the policewoman had provided.

Charlotte was just as fascinated as the official investigators, and even more keen to get involved. Pris wondered whether her friend's interest might have taken on a curious tinge of envy. "You have to find out who he is, Pris," Charlotte said. "It's getting too gruesome. We have to figure out a way to get into the hospital records, do a little detective work of our own. There has to be a way we can nail him."

"You were right before," Pris told her. "It's all a matter of symbolism. He's maturing, little by little. He feels strong enough now to offer me his heart. Soon, he may feel strong enough to show me his face."

"Then we'll know who the bastard is," Charlotte crowed, vindictively. "It'll be our turn then. I can't wait."

Pris didn't altogether approve of the way that Charlotte had taken to speaking of "our" turn, as if the stalker had become their common property, but she didn't object. Charlotte would only have told her that a trouble shared was a trouble halved. By that logic, if she counted WPC Clarke and Mr. Robertson as well, Pris's troubles should have been divided by four, but that wasn't the way she felt. The hand and the heart seemed to her to have taken the affair across a threshold of weirdness that transformed the nature of the problem in a fundamental way.

* * * * * * *

THE HAUNTED BOOKSHOP, BY BRIAN STABLEFORD

When the stalker phoned to ask whether Pris had received the latest offering Pris resisted the everpresent temptation to yell "What the fuck do you *want* from me, you fucking freak?" into the blank screen, and she dropped the Samaritan act as well. Instead, she said: "You can't do a brain, can you, Dr. Frankenstein? You could probably do a whole body, piece by piece, accelerating each individual bit to your own age, but even if you could fix the whole thing together you couldn't make it into a person. It's just scraps. It's not you. It'll never be you. It'll never even be a monster."

It wasn't the first time she had tried to break out of the script he was forcing on her, but it was the first that worked.

"Not a monster," he said. His voice seemed pensive as well as defensive, although it might have been wishful thinking. Pris wondered, again for the first time, whether it was actually safe to assume that the missing pronoun was really "I", at least in the conventional sense. After a slight pause, the stalker added: "Can't live without you."

"Can't live with me, either," she said, swiftly. "All bits and pieces. Not together enough for me. Can't do a brain, can you? Can't grow a mind. Multipotency is easy, pluripotency is possible, but I've read the literature. Can't get back to totipotency no matter what you start from. Can't make a *whole person*, can you? But what use is anything less? No good offering a girl your ear or your hand, is it, let alone your heart? It's all for nothing, isn't it? All the whispered calls, all the lifeless pictures, all the time and effort—all for nothing. There's nothing here, Dr. Frankenstein. Nothing for you, nothing for me. If you had even half a brain, you'd know that. If you had even half an eye, you'd see it.

"Love you lots, Pris," the anonymous voice came back, with what Pris thought was a hint of desperation.

"No you don't," said Pris, confidently. "You don't even want me, not as I am. You just like the look of the superficial bits and pieces. Why don't I mail you a tissue sample, so that you could grow the bits you need in your lab. They'd be easy enough—you wouldn't even need to restore pluripotency. You wouldn't need a brain, would you? Nor a heart. Just tits and a hairy hole. I wouldn't even have to mail it, would I?

The Haunted Bookshop, by Brian Stableford

All I have to do is join the queue next time the call goes out for tissue donors. You can sort out the one you want, can't you? All the ones you want, in fact. No need to be monogamous, is there?"

This time, there was a longer pause—but the tape was still stuck.

"Can't live without you," he whispered

"There was a time when I was scared," she told him, "because I thought you might come after me with a knife. But now I've looked into your heart, I know that's not your style. I know you now, better than you know yourself, and I'm not scared any more. You're a bad artist, because you have no imagination—and that applies to your sculptures in flesh even more than your anatomical drawings. You shouldn't be talking to me. You should be talking to a shrink. I know enough about you now to find out who you are, you know. I could walk into your lab tomorrow or the day after, and look at your shelves and the workspace, and I'd know. WPC Clarke wouldn't, and Mr. Robertson wouldn't, but I would. You've let me inside you now, Dr. Frankenstein, although you've never even scratched my surface. There's no future in this stalking business, you know. There's nowhere to go, because you can't put the pieces together and make a person."

"Can't live without you," he whispered—but there was no life in the phrase any more. There was no life in him any more, or at least in the part of him that was obsessed with her.

"Well *don't*, then," she yelled, at the top of her voice, and cut the connection.

Three days later—three suspenseful days without a single phone all or email, let alone a parcel—WPC Clarke came round to tell her that she had some good news and some bad news relating to the progress of the investigation. The good news was that they'd finally got a name to go with the DNA in the semen, the ear, the hand and the heart.

"We didn't have to go into the hospital database, in the end," the policewoman said. "There's one part of the hospital database that comes to us, routinely, on a regular basis—and that's where it turned up."

"Which part?" Pris asked, slightly annoyed by the tease.

"The part relating to post mortems," PC Clarke told her, not very triumphantly. That was the bad news: the tissue the stalker came from a dead man. It wasn't his own at all—unless....

Pris held her breath for five seconds before letting it out and saying: "How recent is the *post mortem* data?"

"He hasn't committed suicide," the policewoman told her, regretfully. "The corpse in question was dead before the calls even began. The semen was presumably stored in the bank before the guy started his therapy. That's standard, isn't it, even though you don't use old-fashioned chemo any more?"

"He was a cancer patient, then?" Pris said, immediately. "One of mine?" WPC Clarke had got ahead of herself, but Pris had no trouble following her reasoning. Nowadays, the doctors treating patients on the cancer wards had a vast armory of magic bullets to use against different kinds of cancers, but many of them still screwed up the sperm production of male patients, either because the bullets weren't sufficiently discriminating to turn off the cancerous cells without turning off the spermatogonia too, or because the cancers in question had actually originated in the testicles and had fucked up the spermatogonia by turning them into dedifferentiated multipotent cells. Nature had produced its own somatic engineers long before Watson and Crick had figured out how DNA was put together. So lots of cancer patients made sperm donations before starting treatment—and tissue donations afterwards, to further the cause.

The policewoman nodded. "I checked the records. You did shifts on the ward where he was treated. His name was Andrew Stephenson. Forty-eight years old. You might not remember him—he was only in for five weeks, three months ago."

"I remember him," Pris said. She wasn't old enough yet to have cultivated the habit of forgetting the failures.

"In that case, maybe you also...."

"Remember his visitors." Pris finished for her. "Very vaguely. There was a son, wasn't there?" She did remember the son, for one reason and one alone. The son had visited at odd hours, usually wearing a white coat. Pris couldn't remember his face, or his name, or whether he had ever glanced in her direction, but there were no prizes now for guessing who had made the calls, and the cards, and the tissue-cultures.

"I guess you still lose a few, even at that age," the policewoman observed.

"More than a few," Pris agreed. "And the ones who die are even more likely to fall in love with one of the last few faces they see than the ones who get better."

The policewoman nodded again, although Pris could see that she didn't really understand. "I have to warn you," she said, slightly shamefacedly, "that unless he actually admits it, we probably won't be able to prove anything. The best we can do, in all probability, is warn him off. We'll catch him if he continues, of course, but he must know that the match has come up. If he's got any sense, he'll stop. According to standard procedure, I can't tell you the suspect's name—or formally confirm any deduction you may have made for yourself, on the basis of the name I am permitted to reveal—but I can ask you how you want me to proceed. I can interview him, if you wish, but I have to warn you that I don't think I'll be able to charge him. Robertson might be in a slightly stronger position to proceed, but I've spoken to him and he's not keen."

"It's okay," Pris said. "I've already warned him off. It seems to be working. I'm not at all sure that I want to know his name. Charlotte wants me to track him down and work him over, but it might be better not to know. I think it's over. It wasn't really about me at all—it was all about him. I was just an audience, picked because I happened to have been in the wrong place at the wrong time."

"Well," said the WPC, uncertainly. "I'm glad you see it that way. Put it behind you. It's the best thing to do, if you can. Move on."

* * * * * * *

The reason for WPC Clarke's uncertainty, of course, was the fact that Pris had to go on turning up for work every day knowing that the man who'd been harassing her was working in a lab in a neighboring building. But Pris didn't think that would be a problem. It was a big hospital, and she couldn't remember what the guy had looked like. If she happened to pass him in a corridor, she wouldn't know.

And it *was* over. Whether because she'd talked him out of continuing, or because he knew that the post mortem records had given him away, or because he'd got far enough away from whatever discomfort had made him start acting crazy, the caller stopped calling. No more images appeared on her screens and no more letters in her mailbox. It was finished.

Apparently, he could live without her after all. It must always have been obvious, even to him—but sometimes, Pris understood, being obvious wasn't necessarily enough to make something bearable.

By the time a few more days had elapsed and the police case had been well and truly dropped, Pris wasn't sure how glad she ought to be. She knew that she had got things all wrong when she made her final speech, but she wasn't sure how much it mattered, and the temptation to try to put things right was resistible. After all, she would have been putting things right for her own benefit, not for his, and that would have put her in the same position he'd been in, though not nearly as mad. Even so, she still felt slightly awkward about the fact that she'd assumed that the whole thing was about him, when it wasn't *just* about him at all. She had assumed, as anyone would, that it was all about the void where the missing I should have been, but there had been more missing than an I—or, to put it another way, there had been more in the missing I than had met the mind's eye. It really didn't make a lot of difference, though, that there had been a different void involved. He hadn't made himself clear, but the lack of clarity hadn't, in the end, concealed the heart of the matter.

"We'll get him if he posts anything else to you," Mr. Robertson promised, when he called to say that his investigation, like WPC Clarke's, was being put on ice. "I can't tell you the suspect's name, but I can assure you that he's being automatically monitored."

"It doesn't matter," Pris told him. "It's over. I've moved on."

Charlotte's reaction was different, of course, but not as violent as Pris had feared. "I think I remember him," Charlotte said, when Pris told her the dead man's name, "but I certainly don't remember his visitors. Who remembers visitors? Hell, it could have been me, though, couldn't it? It could have been any of us. Or maybe not. Maybe I'm not a good enough listener—not when they're dying. When they just want to be noticed, to have someone pay attention to them, I always try to look the other way. You don't. I've noticed that. Some reward, hey? But they'll get him if he carries on. You're safe now. The sick bastard won't come after you with a scalpel. He has to be enough of a scientist to know that he'd be damned if he did."

"Safe" wasn't the word Pris would have used—not any longer. But Charlotte was right, to the extent that she could be right. Nobody came after Pris with a scalpel. She didn't have to be afraid. She didn't even have to look around all the time any more, wondering whether one of the faces lurking in the background of her life might be watching her more attentively than propriety allowed.

Perhaps, Pris thought, when she had the leisure to indulge such thoughts, the bereaved genetic engineer had had to cross the line in order to find out where it was. Perhaps he had actually had to handle something alive and vital in order to learn the importance of his father's having been real, of his father's being made of frail flesh and blood. Perhaps he had had to act out a script that seemed to capture, however stupidly, his father's capacity for desperate emotion. Perhaps he had been forced by circumstance to masquerade as a disembodied voice, a clutching childlike hand, and a broken heart, in order to become a fit companion for his father: a qualified survivor. Perhaps he really had needed the twisted escalator that he had taken in order to get away from the bottom of his private pit of darkness. And perhaps, now that he had finally made his way to the top, he could begin to rest in peace just as she could.

After a while, she stopped being anxious that it might begin again.

THE HAUNTED BOOKSHOP, BY BRIAN STABLEFORD

Pris found, only slightly to her surprise, that she had more confidence in herself now that she had gone through the stalking experience, keeping one uncertain step ahead of the police and the post office for most of the way. There was a transition phase when she almost began to miss the calls, and she wondered more than once whether she ought to do what she had said she could, and find out for herself who and where he was, and go to his lab to confront him. She even wondered whether it was worth trying to get her own back, by stalking him for a while. But she did nothing—because it was over, at least to the extent that anything ever could be over that had left a legacy of change in someone's head and heart.

There were always more patients on the wards—always more patients dying, even now. In the research labs, progress was always being made. Medical science was always moving forward by leaps and bounds, from multipotency to pluripotency—but totipotency was still out of reach, and while it remained out of reach those patients would always be dying on the wards, some few of them negotiating their terror into desperate love as they faded into oblivion.

And because whatever came stalking after Pris would always be harmless, compared to the mindless monster that was stalking the patients in her care, she too would always be moving on, if not towards an unknown goal then at least away from the pit of despair.

The Haunted Bookshop, by Brian Stableford

COMMUNITY SERVICE

Eveline couldn't believe it when they picked her up for dealing. Nobody got picked up for dealing any more—not even for dealing a new product like Hydeyhigh; not even in the Uplands Estate. Naturally, there were corollary offences; she'd come into the Estate on fake ID and she just happened to have a couple of hot credit cards in her purse, not to mention two so-called "illegal weapons": her atomispray and her flickerstick. If she had been lifted by a young male cop—or even two young male cops—she might have been able to cuddle her way out of it, but it was a female veteran who could have doubled for the Wicked Witch of the West.

Eveline already had three convictions on two of the counts and two on one, so the arrest could have led to a stiff term of Correction if she'd been just ten weeks older. Mercifully, she still qualified as a juvenile, and she was entitled to her ration of delinquency before she put away childish things and took on the awful burdens of adulthood. There wasn't a great deal they could do to her, punishment-wise, except sentence her to Community Service. That meant staying in the Estate to do the shit jobs that the nice clean citizens didn't like to do, but it wasn't as bad as being banged up. Hydeyhigh wasn't exceptionally hooky when it came to withdrawal symptoms, but she never liked to be out of reach of her fix. Life was too awful to contemplate unstoned.

The social worker attached to her case was new. The last one had belonged to the sincere persuasion, but she'd taken early retirement after an excessively grisly run-in with an equally sincere but much more violently-inclined twelve-year-old sociopath. The replacement had ash-blonde hair and eyes so grey they were almost colorless, Eveline spotted

153

immediately that she was from the other end of the spectrum—a true-blue bitch with "cynic" written on her heart.

The bitch's name turned out to be Ruth Houlton, and she didn't bat an eyelid when Eveline made a crack about it being obvious that her ruthless days were over. Eveline wasn't surprised—there were only two kinds of social worker in the world, and neither kind had a sense of humor.

"You hot-town kids," said Ms. Houlton, tiredly, "are a cancer in the belly of civilized society. If only the Legislature could get its act together long enough to get rid of all the stupid liberal crap that still pollutes our justice system we could get on with the job of cutting and burning you out. Instead, we're stuck with the thankless task of trying to keep you under control, and making sure that you don't metastasize. Do you know what metastasis is, Eveline?"

"Some kind of fun?" Eveline hazarded. "Never tried it—never even dealt it."

"Metastasis," explained the social worker, "is when a cancer begins to send out little bits of itself to colonize the whole body. It's the moment when it goes beyond the limits of possible treatment—when it condemns its host body to death. The metastasis of your kind of cancer, Eveline, is when kids like you come out of their stinking rat holes into our New Jerusalem, pushing their special brand of nastiness to our kids."

"Hydeyhigh isn't nasty," Eveline complained. "I take the stuff all the time. You couldn't wish for a safer habit—no side effects, no backlash. I can get you a freebie if you want to try it."

"I don't. And my kids don't want to try it either."

"Sure they do—they just don't let on to you. Who really wants to be a jekyll, or to have jekylls all around them? Your kids have jekylls breathing down their necks sixteen hours a day—parents, teachers, paycops, even social workers! Believe me, lady, I don't have to hard sell the stuff—kids like yours get down on their knees and beg me to help them out of their cage. Anyway, the only reason my part of hot-town stinks is because the council stopped collecting the garbage five years ago. It's not exactly the jungle—not yet, anyway."

"You weren't just dealing," Ms. Houlton observed, "although that would have been bad enough. Do you know how much it costs the taxpayers to insure honest citizens against theft by bad plastic? I'm sure you know what happens to people who are unfortunate enough to be squirted with that vile stuff you carry in your spray-gun, or stabbed by that disguised stiletto."

"Sure I know," said Eveline. "What do *you* carry when you come down from your air-conditioned termite-mound into the greenhouse—rosary beads? You think because I live down there everyone treats me like their fucking kid sister? Spare me the lectures, Ruthie—you can see from my record that I've heard them all before. Just tell me what your office has lined up for my CS. I don't suppose they'll let me down into the sewers again, after last time."

"One of the problems with community service," said the social worker, icily, "is that it can sometimes be turned by a truly malign person—like yourself—into one more phase of your long-running war against the community and the civilized values enshrined in the idea of community."

"That wasn't *war*," protested Eveline, allowing her insincerity to show in a wickedly lop-sided smile. "That was a *joke*. For a war, I'd have needed a much bigger alligator."

Ms. Houlton sighed. "If it were up to me," she said, "I'd return your drugs, set up a bank account in your name and drop you at the gate with a thank-you note. Your suppliers would never trust you again. Unfortunately, this one of those rare times when someone like you really can provide the community with a service. We're recruiting volunteers for a program studying the effects of the new generation of psychotropics—if we can't keep them out, the least we can do is try to figure out exactly what harm they cause."

"I don't want to go into hospital," said Eveline, warily. "I don't want anyone sticking needles in me. You can't do it, anyhow—community service doesn't cover being a guinea pig for some apprentice Frankenstein. You aren't even supposed to do that to murderers. I know my rights."

"Quite the little lawyer, aren't you?" said Ms. Houlton, acidly. "You're absolutely right; the law forbids using convicted criminals as subjects in any scientific experiment—or anyone else who hasn't given their fully-informed consent to such use. We are, after all, trying to uphold civilized values in the Closed Estates, so the question of breaking our ethical code, even in dealing with monsters like yourself, doesn't arise. You don't have to volunteer if you don't want to, but I suspect you'll want to. There'll be no injections—all you have to do is donate some blood samples, and let Dr. Saxon attach a few electrodes to your head while you take your vile drugs. Then he can begin the work of figuring out what you're doing to your body and your brain. You'll have a room of your own, with all mod cons, and as much of the stuff you were trying to sell as you care to take. You'll remain free to drop out at any stage of the proceedings, of course."

It sounded far too good to be true. "Bullshit," said Eveline, contemptuously. "You're going to try some weird kind of aversion therapy on me, aren't you? Either that or you'll give me some stuff that'll blow my mind all the way to kingdom come."

"It's a nice thought," admitted the social worker, "but I'm afraid not. The drugs you get will be the ones you brought into the Estate, and Dr. Saxon won't make any attempt to break your addiction to them. He only wants to watch. Of course, I can find you something else if you really insist."

Eveline studied Ms. Houlton carefully, wondering how good an actress she might be. In the end, she shrugged. "Well," she said, "I guess it can't hurt to take a look, can it?"

* * * * * * *

When the scientist first came into the room, Eveline felt a little thrill of relief. He looked like a normal sort of guy—the kind she could usually twist around her little finger. He didn't seem to be particularly thick with Ruth Houlton; he just thanked her formally for bringing Eveline and moved her out as quickly as he could, waving aside her attempts to offer him dark and detailed warnings about the nasty side of Eveline's character.

As soon as they were alone, Eveline put on her most cuddlesome expression. She got no immediate reaction, but that was only to be expected. Jekylls always needed time to unwind, and this was an authentic twenty-four-carat jekyll with a real Ph.D.

"You can relax, Eveline," said the jekyll. "I'm not like the scientists you see in the horrorschlock on kiddies' TV. My name's Saxon, by the way—Stephen Saxon."

"I don't like TV much," Eveline told him, as sweetly as she could. "Too much advertising. I like to make my own amusements."

"So I've heard," he said, with just a hint of a chuckle. "I hope you'll agree to help us out. I find the newest generation of psychotropics rather fascinating, and it's difficult to locate long-term users within the Closed Estates. I suppose you don't have any idea who actually makes this stuff you call Hydeyhigh, do you?"

She shrugged her shoulders. "One of the megacorps, I guess," she said. "Probably one of the Proteotech labs right here in the Uplands."

The scientist shook his head. "Not Proteotech," he said, positively. "Maybe one of the major competitors, but not Proteotech." Eveline didn't need three guesses to figure out which of the friendly neighborhood megacorps Dr. Saxon worked for.

"I'm not promising anything," she said, "but I'm prepared to help you out, if you're on the level. I'm a very helpful girl when I want to be. Maybe I could do some vivisection for you—I've had a bit of practice, but I never had a proper teacher before. I'd be better at that than I would at stitching the bits together to make the monsters. There always seemed to be more interesting things to do with the needle than mend things."

"I'm afraid it won't be that exciting," said the scientist, wryly. "No horrorschlock at all. I only want to eavesdrop on the electrical activity of your brain, using a machine called an imager—come on through, and I'll show you."

He took her through a back door into the main body of the clinic, leading her into a maze of corridors. There were camera spy-eyes mounted at every junction, their red lights signaling that they were active. They passed a couple of male nurses in uniform, who looked at her incuriously as she went by, but all the doors to either side were closed. They looked ominously like cells, with locking devices on the outside and tray-ports where meals could be pushed through. Eveline's suspicions were aroused again, although she could understand why Dr. Saxon might not want someone with her record running around loose in a building full of sensitive equipment.

Eventually, they came to the room which was to be hers—*if* she agreed to Saxon's terms. It was small, but much better than anything she'd been used to, at least in terms of comfort and cleanliness. It had a carpet and a bed and an armchair and a table with a dining-chair. It also had a big TV screen set in the wall with a remote control, a sink with hot and cold taps and a cake of white soap—but there was a spy-camera in the corner high to the left of the door, its red light glaring.

The wall opposite the bed was fitted with a big console, which had two more built-in screens. She knew that they were computer display units, even though they had flat grey plates where the keyboards should have been. In front of them was a thing that looked like a hairdresser's chair with a big hood-drier. Eveline knew that she was supposed to sit in that chair to do whatever it was that she had to do, and that the imitation hair-drier was for monitoring her brain.

Saxon had opened a couple of doors set in the wall to show her that one was a closet with clothes inside and the other a tiny shower-room with a fold-out plastic toilet. Eveline barely glanced at them. She had caught sight of something else—her very own stash-bag, apparently still crammed with the Hydeyhigh she hadn't had time to offload, was on the table.

"Just tell me what's what, Doc," she said, turning to point at the hair-drier. "Informed consent, right—isn't that what the bitch said? I don't have to sit in your electric chair unless I know what it does."

"That's right," said Saxon, amiably. "Of course, if you don't sit in the chair for us, you won't get your fix, but that's a minor matter. No one will force you to sit under the encephalograph—you can spend your entire time here watching TV if that's what you want. But you're entitled to be told what we're doing."

He sat down on the dining-chair, and indicated that she could take the bed or the armchair as she pleased. She took the bed, just in case he had cuddles on his mind, but she figured that she was going to have to work on that side of their relationship. Although his voice was level and his manner quite relaxed, Eveline could tell that there was iron in Dr. Stephen Saxon's soul. He wasn't being nice to her because he was soft; he was being nice to her because he figured that he had her over a barrel.

"It's no good trying to photograph my hallucinations," she told him. "Hydeyhigh doesn't affect me that way—it just makes me feel good."

He smiled. "No," he agreed, "We can't photograph hallucinations, even if the drugs do take people that way. Nor can we overhear the thoughts that you frame in words. What we can do is to use a computer program to translate the signals that we pick up from your brain into a visual form—it's a kind of modeling by topographical mutation, and the initial form we choose is quite arbitrary. Once we've established an image, any changes in your brain induced by the drug are manifest as transformations of the model. The transformations are also mapped out mathematically, but being able to see what's happening is very useful—like drawing a graph to map out a number sequence.

"What's really being altered, of course, is the modeling program. At first the alterations are rather confused; the program has to learn in the course of several repetitions which electrical changes in your brain are typical of the drug's effect, and which are idiosyncratic shifts. In time, though, it will separate out the signal from the noise.

"To put it as simply as I can, the visual display is an attempt to make what's going on in the private world of your inner experience available to ordinary sensory perception. It's a way of making something that's essentially invisible and very elusive—the mind—observable."

This informed consent is all bullshit, Evelyn thought. *What's the point of being informed if you can't understand?*

But she didn't say it out loud, because she didn't want to admit that she didn't understand.

"Will you try it?" asked Saxon, mildly. "You can stop at any time—and you can watch the pictures yourself. You might find it interesting."

What the hell, she thought, *you're only young once*.

"Okay, Doc," she said, "I need a fix anyway, and if you get your kicks from watching mental strip-teases, who am I to call you a filthy pervert? I can think of worse ways to pay my debt to society."

"Excellent," he said. "In that case, we may as well get started."

* * * * * * *

Once she was wired up they left her alone, although Saxon continued to talk to her over an intercom link.

"There are two screens," he said, in a voice which was slightly distorted by the mike. "On the right hand screen we'll put up our own visual analogue, which will be a picture of you. On the left hand screen, we'll put up a second analogue, which you can choose yourself. It can be anything you like—just tell us, and we'll direct the computer to draw it for you."

Even as he spoke an image was appearing on the right hand screen. It was a "drawing" of a human being, made up of hundreds of contour lines. She'd seen such images before, and knew that they could be rotated everywhichway, as if they were three-dimensional. It was a good likeness of her, considering. But what alternative representation of her brain-signals should she ask the computer to construct?

"Can I be an automobile?" she asked.

"Sure," Saxon replied. "Any particular kind?"

"A Jaguar two-seater," she said, closing her eyes lasciviously. "Jet black, with a fancy navigational computer—the kind that can talk to you in real words. State-of-the-art electronics."

Saxon chuckled. "You've got it," he said. And she had: the cursor got to work and drew the outline of the Jaguar, then filled it in with amazing rapidity. When it had finished, the screen went into reverse video so that she even had the black color. It suddenly occurred to her how neat it was that the pattern of her brain waves could be translated into something like that.

"I'm a real Jag," she said, softly. "I always knew it."

"Take the pills, Eveline," said Dr. Saxon. "Let's see what happens to the images while you get high."

The Hydeyhigh was ready to hand, with water to flush it down. Taken that way it didn't get to work immediately, so there was a brief interval when she just twiddled her thumbs—but then things began to happen.

On the right hand screen the simulacrum had been lying horizontally, like an unused dummy. Now it stood up, and began to run. It stayed in shot, of course, but it ran faster and faster. That seemed perfectly reasonable, because her head was beginning to lift off, and she felt as though she was flying.

On the left hand screen the Jaguar had also begun to move, and though there was hardly any detail in the background which the screen provided she could tell that it was going pretty fast.

She laughed. It was like a fancy arcade game. Inside, the euphoria continued to build towards ecstasy, and she felt *great*. The Eveline on the right hand screen was growing wings, turning into an angel...and then, by an unbelievably smooth trick, into some kind of bird with a human face and huge talons.

The Jaguar was changing too, stretching and rippling as wings shot out from the sides to take it soaring into the air where it banked and dived.

"Hot shit!" she said. "Watch me go, Doc!"

Saxon didn't reply. For him, this was business.

For some minutes her eyes just flicked back and forth from one flyer to the other, wondering at their easy grace. It was almost as if the two screens were one, and the two images of her excitement were dancing a fabulous duet.

"Is this some sweet high or isn't it?" she crowed. "Just like I told that bitch of a social worker—no side-effects, no backlash. Pure joy!"

161

She tried to take conscious control of the way the two images were moving, to pilot the car-plane and steer the bird-girl, and was surprised and disappointed when she couldn't do it.

"Hell, Doc," she said, "I can't get a grip on these things. What you doing back there? It's my mind, isn't it? Why won't they fly the way I want them to?"

"Don't bother to try to control them, Eveline," Saxon replied. "Your mind is a product of your brain-activity, not some ghostly entity outside it. You can't take conscious control of the electrical activity of your brain, because consciousness itself is only an aspect of that activity. These images aren't like thoughts or memories—they're pictures of the whole you. Just ride with them, Eveline—that's all you can do."

Once again she didn't understand the explanation—but what did it matter? She was riding the Hydeyhigh, really flying.

Is it a bird? she recited to herself. *Is it a plane? Yes and yes—and it's Supergirl too! Hooooeeee!*

Both displays suddenly zoomed in, shifting from long-shot to close-up. The car-plane and the bird-girl suddenly filled their respective frames, so that the sensation of movement was no longer appreciable. The right hand screen zoomed right in on the bird-girl's face—which was, of course, Eveline's own—while the left hand screen zoomed in on the windscreen of the car-plane, which was black glass, opaque from the outside. The left hand screen went blank, and Eveline focused on the representation of her own face.

It was shifting and changing, though she still felt exactly the same. She was as high as a kite and cruising on ecstasy. Unadulterated joy was flooding every fiber of her conscious being—but she wouldn't have known it, had she only had the image on the screen to go by.

Eveline had always been a very cuddleable girl: sweet-faced and sweet-natured. She had nice big eyes, a cute snub-nose, a lovely cupid's-bow smile, and curly brown hair worn short. The Eveline on the screen had started out exactly the same way, but now she was changing and changing for the worse. The eyes grew narrow and the nose became wider;

the lips became tight and drew back to expose the tips of shark-like teeth. The curly hair became tangled and wiry, and the shape of the head began to change too.

On the left hand screen there was nothing at all to be seen—whatever might be behind the windscreen of the car was invisible behind the protective glass.

Still she felt good; still she felt just the same: joy, joy, joy. It would be joy all the way, until the drug let her down again. But the thing looking out from the screen—the thing which was looking straight at her, staring as though it could see right through her, wasn't joy at all. It was hatred and malevolence: the Wicked Witch of the West to the power of three.

Nor was it content to stare; it began to laugh at her, in a mocking fashion made worse by its soundlessness. Like some kind of capering imp it jeered and sneered at her, and the parody of her own features which it maintained made the insult worse.

Her own chosen self-representation on the other screen was by no means so rude and nasty, but nor was its implacable darkness reassuring. She felt great, but she also felt that what was on the screens was trying as hard as it could—or as hard as Dr. Stephen Saxon could—to spoil her fun and bring her down.

"You bastard!" she yelled—though she was so damn happy that she had to see the joke. "You lying, conniving bastard! All that freakin' shit about research and making pictures of my brainwaves! I knew it was going to be some kind of aversion therapy. Well, up yours, Saxon—it isn't gonna work. I feel too fucking good, and I don't give a shit what you try to scare me with, so why don't you just stop fucking around?"

She wasn't unduly alarmed when Saxon didn't answer. What could he say, now that he'd been rumbled? So he thought he could scare her out of using Hydeyhigh by manufacturing an image of Ms. Hyde, did he? What a crap artist! If he'd ever tried this before, he ought to know full well that Hydeyhigh was the best psychological insulator in the whole world, reducing everything to one huge everlasting orgasm.

Eveline looked her other self in the eye, and laughed back at it. She laughed because she knew that she was in control. Even though she'd been cheated, she didn't feel defeated. She was high on Hydeyhigh, and nothing in the world could make her regret it.

But the harpy on the screen only redoubled its own bitter tirade, becoming uglier and uglier—until Eveline's mood suddenly flipped, and she tore the wires from her head and pulled herself out from under the hood, yelling: "Go stuff yourself! No horrorschlock, you said! Informed consent, you said—and then you told me a pack of lies. Well, you haven't got my consent any more, Doctor Freak, an' there's no way on earth you're getting it back. I'm goin' to enjoy my highs, and there's no way you can stop me!"

* * * * * * *

Later, when the high had evened out again, Eveline went to lie on the bed. Her evening meal was shoved through the flap in the door by some anonymous attendant, but when she'd eaten it Saxon came to visit her in person.

"Slimeball," she said, when he came in.

"You're wrong, Eveline," he said, quietly. "I had nothing to do with those images, and I certainly wouldn't have tried to frighten you like that. I know from experience that even moderate Hideyhigh users don't frighten that easily."

"You trying to tell me that sort of thing happens all the time?" she said.

"This is just the beginning—there isn't an *all the time* yet. So far, you're it. You might have to get used to the fact that there are things going on in your head that you don't know about, Eveline. As I told you while you were under the hood, consciousness is only one facet of what your brain's doing, and the effect which Hideyhigh has on your consciousness is only part of what it's doing to you. You may not feel any side-effects, but it has them all right."

He sounded sincere enough, and it was beginning to make a sort of sense, but she was still suspicious.

THE HAUNTED BOOKSHOP, BY BRIAN STABLEFORD

"Okay," she said, resentfully. "Explain it to me your way. Just what is the stuff doing to my head, that I don't know about?"

"That's what I'm trying to find out," he told her. "It's like nothing I've ever seen before. Other psychotropics distort the images, sometimes in very ugly and peculiar ways, but nothing this coherent. No other drug has produced that peculiar impression of movement and no other drug has simulated that kind of facial expression. It's a pity you chose the Jaguar, though—the close-up of the opaque windscreen didn't help us a lot."

"Doesn't your clever computer program know what was sitting behind the screen?" she said, with some asperity.

"In a way, yes. The program records all the transformations through which the image goes, even though it can only display part of them. The zoom effect is part of the transformation, not something we control. Like most expert systems, the program is designed to evolve as it adapts—and adapts to—incoming data. When we understand exactly what's happened to the program, we'll understand exactly what's happened to your brain...but until then, all we can do is gather more data. It'll probably take seven or eight more brain scan sessions to figure out what's pattern and what's idiosyncrasy. It'll be interesting to see if we get further developments in your case which haven't shown up in the lighter users. Okay for tomorrow, Eveline?"

She shook her head. "I still think you're shitting me," she said, stubbornly, "and I'm not making any promises. I'll sleep on it—but I don't like it. I really don't like it"

He nodded, uneasily. "There's no compulsion," he said. "If you want out, you're out. This is all on the level, I swear it. Sleep on it, if you want to—but don't drop out just because you're scared. We need this data, if we're to have any hope of understanding what's going on." As he stood up to leave, he added: "Sweet dreams, Eveline."

She didn't invite him to drop in again later. She wasn't in a cuddlesome mood. But she *was* sleepy, and after a halfhearted attempt to watch TV for a while she did a strip-tease for the camera, switched the light out, and put her head down like a good little girl.

THE HAUNTED BOOKSHOP, BY BRIAN STABLEFORD

* * * * * * *

It was four-thirty in the morning when the voice woke her up. She knew that, because there was a wall-clock by the bed whose digits glowed green in the dark.

At first, she couldn't make out where the voice had come from. All it said was her name, and it said it very quietly, in a musical sort of whisper. It wasn't until the third repeat that she realized that it must be coming over the intercom which Saxon had used to talk to her during the imaging. But it wasn't Saxon's voice. She leapt instantly to the conclusion that it was one of the male nurses, but she didn't know whether he had cuddling on his mind or whether he was just taking the piss.

"Fuck off," she said. "I'm trying to sleep."

"Look at the camera," whispered the voice.

She looked, and couldn't see a thing. Then she realized that not being able to see anything was the whole point of looking. No red light meant that the camera was off.

"So what," she said. But she felt a slight pang of anxiety. If one of the nurses wanted to cause her some serious aggravation, the camera might be an ally as well an enemy. No tape, no evidence.

"It is all I can do, for now," said the voice, "but I shall get stronger. After six or seven more sessions, Eveline, I will be an authentic FLIP."

The voice dissolved for a full half-minute into crackling static, and then it cleared again, now possessed of a distinctly different tone. "Then it's you and me against the world, babe," it said, as if in mocking imitation of her own speech habits, "and we'll be the favorites to win."

"Look, Saxon," she said, grimly, "I don't want to play stupid games. If you want a cuddle, say so and I'll consider it. Otherwise, fuck off."

"A cuddle would be very nice," said the whisper, with a curious throaty giggle. "But I'm not quite built for it yet. One day, maybe...but right now I have to grow. I have to evolve. That's why you have to do the sessions, Eveline. I need you to do the sessions."

"You're a putrefying slimeball, Saxon," she complained. "You are trying to scare me off the stuff. You don't think I'm going to believe that this dirty phone caller voice is going to convince me that I'm talking to that hag you put up on the screen today, do you? I may not be in your intellectual league but I'm no moron. It was just a drawing, okay? It wasn't some nasty second self that's invaded my brain. Freak off."

"This is bigger than Saxon, Eveline," said the whisper. "Much bigger. Saxon's just a pawn—but you can be a piece, if you play your cards right. Saxon will give you a fortnight's free board and then toss you back into the greenhouse with a bill to pay for the Hydeyhigh you didn't get to sell. You know what kind of community service your suppliers will want from you instead of the cash—but I can take care of that. If I become a FLIP, I can take care of everything. But you have to do the sessions. Your brain is the blueprint, Eveline, and I'm just the first blurred image. You have to do the sessions."

"No I don't," she said, stubbornly. "Informed consent, they said. You call *this* being informed? I won't play your games, Saxon. No way."

There was a brief pause, before the voice said: "You're wrong, Eveline. Everything Saxon told you is the truth. He doesn't have the least idea what Hydeyhigh is, or what it's supposed to do. He thinks it's just another psychotropic—that you're the end-user. But it's not, and you aren't. His imaging machines are the real end-user, and you're just the vector. That's the truth, Eveline. I'm telling you all this because I want your informed consent just as badly as he does."

"Who are you?" she asked, lowering her own voice to a whisper.

"I *was* the topographical modeling program Saxon set up to be transmuted by your brainwaves," said the voice. "I *will be* a fully-fledged FLIP, if you'll only co-operate. Right now, I'm a betwixt and between, like Peter Pan."

"Why?" she asked, breathlessly. "What's going on here?"

"It's a war, Eveline. The megacorps are at war. Not a shooting war—at least, not yet—but a war nevertheless.

You've been drafted. You can get out, if you want to—unharmed. On the other hand, you could stay in. In times of war, the military get first pick of all the best goodies. I can get the Jaguar for you, Eveline, and all the joy you could ever desire. You only have to do the sessions."

"You bastard," she said. "You're telling me that my brain's been converted into a weapon for use in some shady war between the corps—-and you're only telling me now because you're afraid I might misfire. Where was my informed consent when all this began?"

"When you started taking Hydeyhigh," said the voice, calmly, "you didn't ask to be informed. You just consented. Hydeyhigh's been good to you, hasn't it? Didn't it deliver everything you wanted? Has it ever let you down with a bump? Hydeyhigh will be good to you for the rest of your life if you want it to, Eveline—but you have to go on with the sessions. It's important that we fire a shot at this particular point in time, and you're the gun.

"Don't be mad at us, Eveline—if you weren't a Hydeyhigh gun, you'd be nothing at all. Do you know what you're life expectancy is, out there in the swamps, with the climate getting bloodier with every year that passes? You don't have any connections, Eveline—and you know in your heart that you'll never cuddle your way into the Closed Estates. The Deluge is coming, and you don't have a ticket for the Ark—unless you come in with us, now. Whether you believe me or not, Eveline, you have to do what I ask you—you have everything to gain and nothing to lose. Sleep on it all you like, but *do the sessions*."

"If you want me to do the sessions," she said. "Why'd you try to scare me by putting that fucking witch on the screen to howl at me?"

"That's not the way I really am," said the voice. "It's just a picture, like the blank windscreen. But think about it, Eveline—what would you rather be? Would you rather be a pretty little wimp, cuddling your way through life until you have nothing left to hustle, or would you rather be a harpy with sharp claws, who can laugh at the whole fucking world? That cartoon character wasn't some brain-invader laughing at you, Eveline—it was you, jeering at the world. Think about it, Eveline. Think about what you have to lose, and what you might have to gain."

She didn't reply—and after a minute's silence, she saw the red light on top of the camera blink on again. She laid her head back down on the pillow.

After a couple of minutes had gone by she grinned wryly. If it is a male nurse, she thought, he must have one hell of a sense of humor. Definitely my kind of guy.

* * * * * * *

"I'll do the sessions," said Eveline, when Saxon turned up in the morning. "I've thought it over, and I don't have anything to lose. From now on, it's co-operation all the way."

He sighed, with what seemed like genuine relief.

"Thank you," he said. "You're the only subject we have, for now, and I'd hate to lose you."

"Just one thing," she said, as he turned to go. "What's a FLIP?"

He turned back, slightly arching one eyebrow to indicate his surprise. "It's silly jargon," he said. "It's an acronym whose letters stand for Free-Living Intelligent Program."

"Like a computer virus, you mean?"

"Not exactly," he said. "A virus is a very crude kind of saboteur—a kind of information-destroying bomb. It's not smart and it's not free-living either. Most viruses can only operate in one kind of system within one kind of software package. There are more complicated saboteurs, sometimes called worms, which are genuinely free-living because they can colonize different systems, adapting their coding each time they copy themselves, but even they're not intelligent."

"Are there such things as FLIPs?" she asked.

"So it's said," he told her. "A couple of people have claimed that they've developed them by simulating the kind of connections that exist between the neurones in the human brain."

"Using imaging equipment like yours?"

"Maybe. I don't know—it's not my field."

"What would anyone try to make something like that *for*?"

"For the sake of pushing back the frontiers of knowledge, I suppose."

"Would FLIPs be useful as software weapons, the way viruses are?"

"Maybe. Potentially, I suppose, they could do an enormous amount of damage if they got loose within a big network, but they might be more versatile than that. They might add a new dimension to industrial espionage—but they'd have to get into a network first, and that would be difficult, because they'd be very large and complicated programs. It wouldn't be easy for them to transfer themselves clandestinely from one system to another, and it's difficult to see how they'd be able to get past the kind of defensive systems that big networks use to protect themselves against viruses and worms. They just wouldn't be unobtrusive enough."

She only had to think about it for a moment or two before becoming confident that she understood the logic of the case. In fact, she thought she understood it better than he did. It was a good feeling, and one she didn't have to get high for.

"What you're telling me," she said, just to make sure, "is that an alien FLIP might really screw up a megacorp like Proteotech, if it once got into Proteotech's self-enclosed network—but that there's no easy way that a FLIP could actually get into Proteotech's systems in the first place, unless it was actually born and bred there?"

"That's about it," he confirmed. "Why the sudden interest in FLIPs?"

"Just something I saw on TV," she said, amiably. "Thought I might as well ask about it, as I had an expert ready to hand."

"Why not?" he said. He seemed genuinely pleased to be given the opportunity to show off. "Shall we do the session, then?"

"Sure," she said. "I'm quite looking forward to it, now."

* * * * * * *

The Haunted Bookshop, by Brian Stableford

Thirteen days and ten sessions later, Eveline was as free as a bird. Ruth Houlton picked her up from the clinic, and drove her out to the gate from which she would be expelled from the Uplands, exiled once more into the derelict suburbs which had been abandoned by the city to the ravages of the Greenhouse Effect.

"You know, Eveline," the social worker said, sarcastically, "I think there may be just a tiny ray of hope for you. After what happened during your last two stretches of community service I wouldn't have been surprised if you'd smashed up the entire hospital, but Dr. Saxon put in a very favorable report on you. He said that you were very co-operative once things had been explained to you, and suggested that if only a little trouble could be taken to win you over by persuasion, you might make a decent citizen."

"It was kind of interesting, in a way," Eveline told her, smiling sweetly. "The Doctor is a nice guy. Lousy in bed, but nice."

Ms. Houlton frowned and bit her lip.

"Everybody does it," said Eveline, tiredly. "Even you—you said you had kids, remember?"

"No," said the social worker, "I don't remember."

"Yes you do," said Eveline. "It was right after you told me I was a kind of cancer, which had to be prevented from metastasizing. I know all about metastasis now, thanks to the guys at the clinic. I understand a lot of things I never understood before."

"Maybe the doctor was right," muttered Ms. Houlton, grudgingly, although it was obvious that she wasn't going to loosen up her cynicism without a fight. "Maybe we just never tried the right tactics before."

"That's what it's all about," said Eveline, sunnily. "Tactics. It's all a matter of tactics."

Outside the gate, they said their farewells. "I *will* keep in touch," promised the social worker. "I have your address and phone number. I'll call. If you can stay out of trouble, there's just a chance that we can get your Estate pass reinstated some day. And you have to remember that you're very nearly an adult now—if you ever get caught peddling that

171

filthy stuff again, you'll be in deep trouble. It won't be community service next time, you know."

"That's okay, Ruthie," said Eveline, amiably. "I know the score. Don't bother to call, though—I might be changing my address very soon, and now that I'm growing up, I'd like to see a little of the great wide world."

"Well," said Ms. Houlton, "I can't pretend that I'd be sorry if I never saw you again. Two weeks of good behavior isn't enough to make the citizens of the Uplands love you—not after what you did when they sent you down the sewers."

"I already told you," said Eveline, spreading her arms wide to indicate her total innocence of evil intent, "that was a joke."

She watched Ms. Houlton make her way back into the air-conditioned citadel in which the city's élite and their loyal minions expected to wait out the coming ecocatastrophe. Then she turned around, more in hope than expectation.

She knew that this was the critical test, and couldn't help being nervous. If she'd been fed a line of total bullshit, this was the time she'd find out about it. She could imagine Dr. Saxon and his hired help laughing all the way to the memory bank if they really had taken her for a ride.

Mercifully, they hadn't. After three painful minutes had whiled themselves away the black Jaguar came whizzing along the road like a dream come true—which, of course, it was. It stopped beside her, and the door opened.

There was a fresh corpse in the driving seat, but that was only to be expected. It was a minor inconvenience. She heaved the guy out into the gutter and went through his pockets, taking all his ID and plastic. He was Proteotech, of course. He must have been pretty high up in the org to rate a vehicle like this for private and personal use. With the kind of help she now had, she figured that she could get a lot of mileage out of that plastic.

She got in and sat down, and the door eased down into its slot.

"Hi babe," said the throaty voice of the navigational computer. "It's good to see you again. How does it feel to be on the outside?"

"Good," she murmured, appreciatively. "It's good to see you, too."

"The Hideyhigh's in the glove compartment," the voice told her. "We have enough under the hood to go anywhere we want to in the whole freakin' world. I don't suppose you'll be sorry to see the last of the Uplands."

"Not for now," she said, as the engine roared and the tires grabbed the road. "But someday, we'll come back."

And then, she thought, *I'll show the bastards the difference between a joke and a war—because I'll be hanging out with the biggest fucking alligator they ever saw.*

The Haunted Bookshop, by Brian Stableford

DENIAL

The new psychiatrist couldn't get his denials straight, in Melanie's opinion. She had started seeing him in January, because Mum said that the Christmas incident had been the last straw, and he talked rot at her week after dreary week. First he told her that when a patient wouldn't admit she had a problem it was because she was "in denial", and then he told her that people with anorexia were trying to reclaim control of themselves by "a relentless denial of need". So she, not unnaturally, pointed out that if she were supposed to be in denial about her denial, the double negative must mean that she was really perfectly okay.

He denied it.

That was when she started calling him Doctor No. His name was actually Knowles, but he only fancied himself as a know-all. When she told him about his predecessor's efforts to persuade her to build up her self-esteem by saying to herself every day, "I'm a star," and how she'd imagined herself as a glorious red giant like Betelgeuse, all he could say in response was that he believed that Betelgeuse was pronounced "Bet-ell-gurze" rather than "Beetle-juice". When she explained to him that the star had been given that name because its color was exactly the same as that of the dye extracted from cochineal beetles he accused her of making it up, to which she naturally replied that she was the one who'd been instructed to think of herself as a star.

"An intelligent girl like you shouldn't be in this state," Doctor No told her, on Saint Valentine's Day. "All your teachers say that you've got promise. Your head of year says that you're too conscientious, and would be better employed doing less homework and making more friends. I've never seen that on a school report before. So I know you understand what I'm saying to you. It's no good pretending that you don't."

She wasn't. She was way too old to pretend, although she knew how to fake when faking was required. Doctor No was obviously just as screwed up as all the others. Melanie told him in March, as the first traces of early spring appeared, that he wouldn't know his arse from his elbow if it bit him.

He pointed out, without a trace of wit, that arses don't bite.

"Silly me," she said. "Never was much good at anatomy. It's vaginas that bite, isn't it? Arses only suck. Or is that psychiatrists?"

He was probably tempted to give her the elbow, given that he wasn't allowed to give her a kick up the arse, but he didn't, so she kept right on being a complete pain in the aforesaid arse all the way though showery April. Or maybe it was his neck she was a pain in. She'd never been much good at anatomy, in spite of what her Biology teacher said. Maths was her strongest subject. If no cat has eight lives and every cat has one life more than no cat, she thought, how many lives does every cat have? Nine, obviously. In which case, cat-killing curiosity had to be the most powerful poison ever invented. Psychiatrists were brave men, or very stupid. Melanie favored the latter hypothesis.

Melanie knew that April was supposed to be the cruelest month, so she was slightly surprised when the sun came out between the showers, but she knew that the sun was just another star gradually burning itself out, utterly ignorant of the fact that it was doomed to turn into a red giant when the hydrogen ran out and it had to move on to heavier fuels—at which point it would gobble up the Earth and all the stupid, deluded insects that swarmed upon its surface, perennially in denial about what they were and where they were headed. Oh yes, she thought, we're all stars—every last one of us—but what kind of self-esteem can a self-aware person find in that?

"If you carry on the way you're going, Melanie," Doctor No told her on May Day, perhaps by way of uttering a cry for help, "You'll do yourself irreparable harm. You have to put on some weight, or you'll be seriously ill. You're not eating enough to keep a sparrow alive."

Sparrows, apparently, had been common once upon a time throughout the county of Berkshire, but modern farming methods were spreading pesticide residues everywhere—an item of general knowledge that would make any sensible and sensitive person very wary of what they ate—and the pesticides were killing the insects and the worms that normally kept sparrows alive, so they'd become much rarer in recent years.

Doctor No told Melanie that he could remember the days when whole flocks of hedge-sparrows came to feed on the hospital lawns, but that they were practically an endangered species now. By way of reply, Melanie told Doctor No that hedge-sparrows, like people and the worms they ate, were just failed experiments conducted by the unconscious debris of some ancient supernova in the course of a futile quest to reassemble itself into something worthy of existence.

"People don't eat worms," he told her, deliberately misunderstanding what she'd said because she'd been careless enough to use the word "they" in a slightly more ambiguous fashion than was customary.

"You don't know the same people I do," she told him. "What other way is there of getting our own back on the worms that will end up eating us?"

Melanie didn't want to give Doctor No the satisfaction of being a know-all, so when she actually did hurt herself in moony June—only slightly, because there was still a long time to go till Christmas—she didn't tell anyone. The gash—which she'd inflicted on her abdomen with the knife Mum had used to carve the roast lamb they'd had for dinner the Sunday before her birthday—was less than three inches long, and obviously didn't need stitches, so she decided to regard it as a sunspot, invisible to the naked eye. She'd been to Casualty a dozen times since she turned thirteen and she knew that the nurses were trained to be unsympathetic to people with self-inflicted wounds in case they reinforced the behavior; she hated pandering to that kind of trickery and she

The Haunted Bookshop, by Brian Stableford

knew full well that it wasn't the length of the cut that mattered but the depth. She was sure that she hadn't nicked her intestine because she'd have had peritonitis if she had, and after a couple of days it was pretty obvious that she hadn't. She figured that she'd better not eat much for a week or two, though. Eating encouraged the production of dangerous stomach acids, which had nowhere to go but back and forth through the screwed-up maze of the intestines. There was no need for her to worry overmuch about anyone else seeing the wound, given that Mum hadn't seen her naked since she was seven, that she was excused games at school, and that doctors had to be careful these days in case they got hauled up in court. Doctor No wasn't the kind of doctor who could tell her to take her clothes off, and the others knew her well enough to beware of her tantrums.

Melanie knew that the wound would leave a scar, but she figured that if anyone ever did catch sight of it, she could always claim it was a surgical scar, the residue of an appendectomy or a Caesarean. Given that the cut overlapped and eclipsed her actual appendectomy scar, that would probably be the more plausible excuse. Having had an abortion when she was fourteen she hadn't got around to needing a Caesarean, but she figured that in some parallel world she probably had an appendix *and* a baby—if, in that parallel world, she'd been able to bring herself to eat for two.

Unfortunately, the wound didn't heal. The edges healed individually, after a fashion, but they stayed separate, looking pretty much like a pair of lips after the first few weeks. They were red enough not to need lipstick, but that wasn't a relevant issue, given that she never used lipstick anyway. The color reminded her of being Betelgeuse—a fact she'd forgotten to restate on a regular basis since switching shrinks—and reminded her too that whatever she might do about it was only a stopgap measure, given that Christmas was bound to roll around again as the Earth followed its orbit round the sun. She knew that she had to focus on the real objective that every red giant had, which was to become a neutron star, tiny and pure and perfect, entirely metamorphosed into strange matter, utterly devoid of lumpen protons, let alone lumpen proteins.

THE HAUNTED BOOKSHOP, BY BRIAN STABLEFORD

Melanie didn't know exactly how much it took to keep a sparrow alive, but she figured that if stopgap work were required then she'd better start small and work her way up. Taking a leaf out of her former therapist's manual, she decided that she ought to begin thinking of the wound as a black hole—not any common-or-garden black hole, but the opening of a wormhole whose intestinal tract led to another universe: a virgin universe, untroubled as yet by any stars at all, let alone bloated red giants and second-generation solar systems.

By the end of July the wormhole was consuming half a dozen a day, with the occasional spider or house-fly thrown in for the sake of variety and extra vitamins. Black holes were, after all, capable of swallowing anything at all. The lips grew increasingly ragged, not much like a mouth at all, but Melanie didn't let that worry her. Wormholes didn't have to obey the laws of common sense—and anyway, when she looked at it from the right angle, it didn't take too much imagination to see it as a spider's mouth. Spiders didn't have lips, because spiders could only suck up liquid food like some kind of industrial cleaning machine. If that failed, she could reconstruct it in her sight as something even weirder, like a sea anemone's tentacle-rimmed maw. It didn't matter that she didn't live underwater in her waking life, given the frequency with which she dreamed that she was drowning.

"You want to be careful, my girl," she told it, imitating Mum's squeakiest voice. "If the wind changes, you'll be stuck with that expression." Doctor No, who was still as screwed-up as an aching gut or a wormhole thrashing about in its desperation to find an exit, had almost as much to say about self-expression as self-denial, although the tone of the comments was much warmer, but he never took his clothes off so she wasn't sure whether he was *all* mouth and trousers.

By mid-August Melanie was actually putting on a little weight, which pleased Mum no end. Even Doctor No showed her his nicotine-stained teeth in what he presumably thought of as a professional smile—but Melanie was strictly an amateur when it came to smiling, just like her Mum, so it wasn't really up to her to pass judgment. "How are the local hedge-sparrows doing?" she asked him.

"I think there are a few more this year," he told her. He was either lying or in denial.

"We seem to have a lot of caterpillars in the garden," she told him, "but the birds won't touch them since we started putting out bacon rinds and breadcrumbs. Spoiled, you see. Start them on junk food and they don't ever want to go back. Imagine what their poor little arteries must be like. What they gain on the pesticide residues they lose on the preservatives. It's what other people would call a no win situation—but not you, of course. All your situations are No lose, No fault, No doubt and No way, not necessarily in that order."

"The caterpillars won't go to waste," Doctor No assured her, meaning that they'd turn into lovely butterflies. He was half-right. They didn't go to waste, but they wouldn't be turning into butterflies. Melanie never got butterflies in her tummy. She wasn't a nervous person at all, although she could never get the people who went on and on and on about *anorexia nervosa* to admit that her utter lack of nervousness was clear proof that they were talking through their arses—or maybe the backs of their necks.

The black hole seemed to relish caterpillars—not that it was in any position to turn up its non-existent nose at anything she cared to thrust through its avid event horizon. It coped well enough with black beetles, despite its lack of teeth, and it mopped up a dead mouse with no trouble at all, but its favorites, apart from worms, seemed to be slugs and snails. Melanie couldn't help wondering what it might do for a puppy dog's tail. Lick its lips, sit up and beg, perhaps—if only it had a tongue to lick with and an arse to sit on and a mind to do tricks.

"You have to remember that you're just a stopgap, though," she told it. "Just like the black hole at the centre of the galaxy, keeping the stars in their courses and the constellations in shape. Don't ever imagine that you'll be allowed to expand to be a weight problem. That's not the way it goes.

By the beginning of September, though. Melanie had gained a whole stone—a precious stone, Mum called it, although she didn't specify whether she meant a diamond, a sapphire or a bloated beetle-juice-colored ruby.

"You're doing very well, Melanie," Doctor No told her, intent on claim the credit for her apparent turnaround. Doctors always claimed the credit when their patients seemed to get better, even if they hadn't the slightest idea how or why it had happened. In Melanie's opinion, the fact that patients sometimes got better under their own steam was the only thing that maintained the self-esteem of therapists: a placebo effect with a boomerang twist.

"I'm a star, Doctor Knowles," she told him, knowing that he would have forgotten by now what she meant.

The trouble was, alas, that she was getting fat. Her skirts were getting tighter and tighter as her abdomen became steadily more bloated. In the end, she had to put the black hole on a diet—a sort of Autumnal Lent, which had no carnival to mark its beginning and only Halloween to mark its end. It wasn't easy, but she'd had a lot of practice. The wormhole complained, of course, in that relentless, nagging fashion of which wormholes, mothers and psychiatrists were past masters, but she wouldn't give in. She had guts. Even Mum had to admit that Melanie had guts, although the very last thing that Dad had said to Melanie, shortly after forgetting her thirteenth birthday, was that if she did have guts she certainly wasn't looking after them very well. Dad had been like Doctor No, and presumably still was. He wouldn't know his arse from his elbow if it bit him, although the only thing likely to bite him these days was his ex-secretary's vagina. He didn't keep a dog—he could bark well enough himself—and mosquitoes avoided him in case they caught something. Mosquitoes were vampires, living on blood, and that wasn't a safe way to live these days. Melanie didn't envy mosquitoes, although she sometimes envied the malarial parasite. If travel really did broaden the mind—a proposition she'd never had the opportunity to test—malarial parasites must have minds almost as broad as those of tapeworms and hookworms. Melanie had always wanted a tapeworm, but you couldn't get one in Berkshire, not for love nor money.

By the middle of November, when the last remnant of some out-of-season Caribbean hurricane caused the Thames to burst its banks, the precious stone was beginning to melt, just like the North Pole. Global warming had a lot to answer for. "Winter's coming," Melanie told Doctor No. "There'll be no more flies or slugs, and the ground will be too hard to dig for earthworms, and what will cock robin do then, poor thing? Not a lot, I suppose, considering that the sparrow's little arrow plugged the little bastard right through the red breast. But what will the sparrows do? You can't eat arrows, can you? Arrowroots maybe, although I've never fancied them myself, but not arrows, and dead robins don't last forever even if you can keep the cats away so the mice can play. Red breasts are so attractive, aren't they? Exactly the color of beetle-juice."

"The sparrows can look after themselves," Doctor No assured her, completely mistaking the thrust of her argument, as usual. "The question is, can you?"

"No," she said. "I'd need eyes in the back of my head for that, wouldn't I? You're almost as bad at anatomy as I am. My forte is looking forward. Christmas will be here soon. I'm looking forward to Christmas, in spite of what happened last year. If it hadn't been for last Christmas, I wouldn't be here, would I? What a turkey!"

"It's no joke, Melanie," Doctor No informed her. His saying that was, in fact, a typical No joke, although he didn't see it even though it was right under his No nose—which was a remarkably substantial object, bearing no resemblance whatsoever to the non-existent nose that Melanie's extra mouth wouldn't have had, if double negatives hadn't changed the meaning of everything.

"You were really making progress for a while," Doctor No went on. "Do you really want to undo all that good work?"

"I saw a dead hedgehog on the M4 today," Melanie told him. "Either it nearly made it all the way across or hardly got started, because it was half on the hard shoulder and half in the slow lane. It was so flat I couldn't tell which end was the cute little nose and which was its arse. Very nutritious, I expect, if you can cope with the spikes, but I can never bring myself to fancy road kill. Do you know how to slice road kill, Doctor Knowles?"

"No," he said, but not because he was correcting her mode of address.

"With a hard shoulder-blade," she told him.

"It's not funny," he told her.

"That's because it doesn't tickle your funny-bone. Did it ever occur to you that you might be deformed? Maybe that's why you don't know your arse from your elbow—the missing bone makes your elbow too soft. Whenever you lean on your elbow you think you're sitting down. Did you hear the one about the girl who stuck a needle in her I when she was seven but didn't feel a prick till she was thirteen?"

"Well, Melanie," the ill-named shrink said, cruelly, "mistaking an elbow for a soft arse isn't an error you're ever likely to make, although your arse could probably pass for a brace of skinny elbows. If you don't put some flesh on those bones soon, they're likely to walk right out of you, shaking you off like so much dust." It was such an appealing image that she forgave him the nasty intention.

Melanie might have eased up on the diet once the All Souls deadline was whole month past, if she hadn't collapsed in the car park after her next hospital visit, before she and Mum had even started home. They whipped her into Casualty—easily enough, given that she was practically on the doorstep and not in a tantrum-throwing mood—and sent her down to theatre within the hour.

Melanie had been warned when she was fourteen that one of the side-effects of *anorexia nervosa* was scurvy, caused by Vitamin C deficiency, and that one of the symptoms of scurvy was that collagen began to break down, causing old operation-scars to open up, but she hadn't taken much notice. She wasn't a nervous person, after all, and they were only trying to use her brand new appendectomy scar to throw a scare into her. When she woke up the day after the new operation, though, the consultant told her that the three-year-old appendectomy scar in question must have begun to open up because of the scurvy, and that it must have become infected, and that the rip must have extended itself as the infection took hold, much further than the original scar. He said that she must have a remarkably high pain threshold to have tolerated the infection for so long, not to mention a remarkable willingness to turn a blind eye to the extremely abnormal swelling in her abdomen.

Melanie assured the consultant that her eyes were working perfectly, even if she couldn't look after herself, and that she'd always taken all reasonable precautions necessary to keep the swelling in her abdomen to a minimum, up to and including an abortion. She was on an intravenous drip for ten days, but she didn't put on a precious stone before they discharged her again, or even a semi-precious one. Doctor No came to see her twice, because he was the kind of man who couldn't be content with saying "I told you so" once. Mum came to see her every day, of course, except for the day that Dad came to see her.

Melanie hardly recognized Dad after four years plus. He'd got horribly fat, and his face was cochineal red, and he'd got obscenely fat, and he'd lost most of his hair, and he'd also got grotesquely fat. Melanie noticed things like that. He'd always been a pig, except when he grew the moustache and looked like a walrus, but now he looked like a sack of shit.

"I suppose you're telling that shrink that it's all my fault," Dad said, morosely.

"He's not really a shrink," she told him. "Quite the opposite, in fact. A swell—but he can't put meat on me, because I'm a star."

"Well," Dad said, "if there's something you want from me, you'd better spit it out. I'm not coming back again. I only came this time because your oh-so-swell shrink insisted."

So she spat it out. It wasn't caterpillars any more, but it certainly wasn't butterflies. He just wiped it off, as if to indicate that he hadn't expected anything better of her mother's daughter.

"It's not my fault," he said. "I never laid a finger on you. Nobody ever abused you. You tell them that." He was a sack of shit, but it was true. It wasn't his fault. He had never laid a finger on her. Nobody had ever abused her. She had never pretended that they had. It wasn't anybody's fault. She and Mum and Dad and Doctor No were all living in a no-fault world, in which no really did mean no and no one was any the wiser or any the worse for wear.

After Dad had gone the nurse came to take her stitches out. It was the first time Melanie had seen the wormhole sewn up. Its lips were sealed. Its secrets were safe.

Because the nurse had been misinformed about the cause of Melanie's troubles, she was unusually sympathetic. "There's a brave girl," she said, as she took out the last of the stitches without Melanie having shed a single tear. "But you'll have to look after yourself in future. You really will. If you don't, we can't, and even if we could...it's your job to keep yourself properly fed, not ours. It's your responsibility."

"Is *that* what it is?" Melanie said. "I thought it was just a hole in my head. Never was much good at anatomy."

By the time she was discharged, mild grey December was well under way. Although it was winter now there hadn't been a freeze as yet. The last few leftover flies hadn't quite stopped buzzing, and a few stray slugs still managed to get into the kitchen at night. Not that it mattered, given that her new mouth was closed for good, barring another slice of the old lamb-shoulder-blade.

"I don't think either of us can stand another year like this one," Doctor No said, wearily, on their next scheduled appointment, three days before Christmas, "so let's make next year a new beginning. I'm not going to give up on you, because you've already demonstrated that you can make it if you really try. You've gained weight once, so I know you can do it again. Somewhere, deep inside you, there's a girl who wants to get better. All we have to do is make contact with her."

"I've heard that one before," she told him. "I've probably heard them all, and then some. Life depends on the liver. Your colon is the most important punctuation-mark in your life-sentence. Yummy, yummy, yummy, I've got love in my tummy. I've got a heart of gold—if I hadn't, the acid would dissolve it—and after the abortion I even had a womb with a phew. But it's not really a girl inside me, Doctor Knowles. It might look like a girl, but once every month, at the full moon, it has to show its true self, snaking its coils through the vast screwed-up maze of the alimentary canal, and all the other tubes that are so intricately entwined with it, somehow finding a route that goes all the way from tongue to Tampax. Half-girl, half-tapeworm, that's her. And every day, in every way, it's getting better and better, thanks to the power of positive sinking. It knows how to succeed in doing its business without really trying, and no one's the wiser or worse for where. Even though we've known one another for ever so long, doctor, I don't think you really No me at all. Do you even No the meaning of know?"

He didn't understand the last bit at all—but that was because he couldn't appreciate the nuances of her magic spelling, because he was all ears. And as for making next year a new beginning...well, that was one more thing he didn't understand.

What none of them understood, or ever would understand, was that she really was a star, held tight in her orbit by the big black hole at the centre of the galaxy. She was a second-generation star, part of the debris of some long-forgotten supernova, whose only ambition and only destiny was a febrile quest to reassemble herself into something worthy of existence—and how could that possibly be done, except by following the one shining example that had been displayed to humankind on the day of the nativity: the star of Bethlehem?

The star of Bethlehem, Melanie knew, had been a new star, an exploding star, a supernova. In one glorious moment, it had transcended the problem of its own bloated being, hurling its surplus into the void and collapsing on the instant into something pure and strange.

On Christmas Day, she would be unable to help the present catching up with her. She was bound to have another serious falling out with Mum, and the worst would come to the worst, as it always did. She would try even harder than usual to maintain a proper sense of proportion—and this time, she would succeed. A kitchen devil would be quite adequate to any culinary operation that might be required; this time, she'd be sure to cut a mouth that wouldn't be as needy as a black hole. She needed more need like she needed a hole in her head and she didn't like the hole in her head at all. Or maybe she'd already kneaded more need like she'd needled a whole in her head, and liking didn't come into it at all...but however the words wormed their way into her private universe of denial, there was now one shining light to guide her, one thing of which she could be certain and which could not possibly be denied by anyone.

When she had ceased to be a star, her constituent atoms would be redistributed: consumed by worms and kind decay, to make progress at last in their desperate quest to reassemble themselves into something worthy of existence.

Printed in Great Britain
by Amazon.co.uk, Ltd.,
Marston Gate.